I0557444

When Stars TAKE FLIGHT

by

Bethany Maines

Blue Zephyr Press
2661 N. Pearl, #360
Tacoma WA 98407

This book is a work of fiction. Names, characters, and incidents are products of the author's imagination or are used fictiously. Any resemblance to actual events or persons living or dead is entirely coincidental.

Copyright © 2018 by Bethany Maines

All rights reserved, including the right to reproduce this book or portions thereof in any form whatsoever.

Cover art by **LILT**.

ISBN-10: 1-7320863-0-3
ISBN-13: 978-1-7320863-0-2

Galactic Dreams

What if somewhere out in the future a heroine must save a girl who is already dead?

What if on a planet with no sky a woman with no wings could fly?

What if on a lonely moon there was a prince who could only be rescued by the girl who came to kill him?

Welcome to the universe of Galactic Dreams, where fairy tales are reimagined for a new age—the future. In each Galactic Dreams novella you'll find an old tale reborn with a mixture of romance, technology, aliens and adventure. But beware, a perilous quest awaits behind every star and getting home again will depend on a good spaceship, true love, and maybe just a hint of magic.

Galactic Dreams is a unique series of science-fiction novellas from Blue Zephyr Press featuring retellings of classic tales from different authors, all sharing the same universe, technology, and history.

We hope you enjoy this adventure.

Table of Contents

WHEN STARS
TAKE FLIGHT

PART I:

Of Toads, Birds, & Dresses

One night, while she lay in her pretty bed, a large, ugly, wet toad crept through a broken pane of glass in the window, and leaped right upon the table where Thumbelina lay sleeping under her rose-leaf quilt. "What a pretty little wife this would make for my son," said the toad, and she took up the walnut-shell in which little Thumbelina lay asleep, and jumped through the window with it, into the garden.

Hans Christian Andersen, Thumbelina

Chapter 1:

Lina Tum-bel dangled by her ankles and considered her life. When she had accepted the position of ambassador to Earth's wayward former colonies, she had really thought there would be a lot more pomp and circumstance and a lot less brutality and mayhem. And a lot less toad people. Also, and not for nothing, a lot less toad-person crotch. If she was to be suspended by her feet, it seemed totally unnecessary that her face be at their groin level. It was like listening to a bunch of talking penises.

Penis number one was arguing for slitting her throat and cannibalizing her ship for parts. Penis number two was advocating for selling her and her crew to the nearest slave trader. And Penis number three was arguing for a combination of plans one and two, but with more rape and torture. There appeared to be some general resistance to the rape plan based on the fact that she and her crew were all so malformed and hideous. But also, why did Penis Three have to be *that* guy? She concurred that one should never be *that* guy, but thought *hideous* was a bit strong considering that their captors had protruding googly eyes, wide gaping mouths, bald heads, skin tinged to a greenish gray, and no necks to speak of—just shoulders melding seamlessly to ears.

After Earth's first interplanetary alliance had fallen to civil war, the planets and far bases, populated by enterprising human colonists, had been left on their own. Now, over seven hundred years after the first alliance failed, the people of Earth were once again reaching out to their former colonies, only to discover that their cousins no longer looked the same. Humans across the galaxy had used genetic manipulation to adapt to their far-flung homes. On a theoretical, diplomatic level, Lina found this acceptable, practical, and most likely necessary. On a personal level, she was finding the ick factor a bit stronger than expected.

Lina's mission was to visit the former children of Earth and bring them into the new interplanetary alliance. Aside from a few hiccups and misadventures, previous planets and bases had been mostly receptive. The bases in Nebula Six were proving to be deviations from the norm.

She twisted gently on her chain. As the mission leader, she'd been given a gold chain and ankle cuffs. She supposed that was a nice thought? She surveyed her fellow Terrans on their rusting steel chains. Poor Captain Aaro Carbanado was attempting to breathe through his own nose blood. First Mate Althea Fina looked as though she was about to pass out, and Petty Officer Edna McCoy was probably working on a cunning plan to blow something up. When it came to explosions, Edna could always be relied upon.

But was unconstrained detonation really the way to go in this situation?

Lina twisted again and surveyed the array of penises presented to her. They were all wearing some sort of codpiece. Only by cranking her neck up or down could she see more of their anatomy or clothing.

The guard next to her was wearing a full helmet and carapace that covered him from the shoulders up. The armor over his chest was well-defined, and the size of his codpiece was enough to make her wonder if genetic engineering had been deployed to affect other parts of their anatomy. The chain spun her the other way, and she decided that the guard was either naturally gifted or padding his codpiece.

She and the crew were dangling from an armature connected to a twenty-foot platform that hovered over the floor of a cavernous hanger deck. She had emerged from her ship—the *Tempest*, still moored a hundred feet above her head—and found herself stepping onto the floating platform to have what she had hoped would be a civil conversation with someone calling himself a prince. What had ensued was an ambush that resulted in the remaining crew locking themselves into the ship while she, the captain, the first mate, and the petty officer had found themselves unceremoniously clapped in chains and hauled up by their ankles. Thank goodness she'd worn pants.

The crew in the *Tempest* had not made any untoward moves as yet, but Lina knew that should matters turn serious, their standing orders were to blast their way out and return with an armada. Due to the vagaries of space travel, however, that process would likely take about three months. And, due the vagaries of her family, the portion of the fleet stationed nearest to their location was helmed by her older brother. Solving this matter here would be a lot more efficient and a lot less embarrassing at the next family gathering.

The argument above her was growing heated. The man-toad they were referring to as Prince, swayed by every new argument and his own waffling, was beginning to anger the others.

"Gentlemen," said Lina, deciding that there had been quite

enough nonsense, "while I appreciate all your plans and, clearly, some have more advantages than others"—there was a pause as they all tried to figure out which plans she thought were which, but she continued on, addressing the head penis—"I think the obvious solution is to send for the queen. She's really the one who ought to make the decisions, don't you think?" She had not yet ascertained whether the queen was the prince's mother or wife, but it didn't take much reading of the room to have guessed that they were all scared of her.

"I think she's right," said the prince.

"Of course you think she's right," snapped another penis, who Lina thought was some sort of cousin to the prince. "You lay flat for anything with mammaries. You need to get with the modern times. Females aren't always right!"

"But usually," said the prince, "they are. Women are just more naturally able to make decisions. I know it's the latest fad to pretend men can have it all, and maybe that's fine for small things, but this is a matter of interbelt diplomacy."

"Interplanetary," corrected Lina. "I keep telling you, we're from Earth."

"Pull my egg sack and try another one," suggested the cousin. "You're all obviously Ránfuglar."

"But their ship doesn't look Ránfuglar," said the prince. "I think we should send for my mother."

"And that," boomed a commanding voice from the far end of the hangar deck, "is the smartest thing you've said today."

The penises parted and Lina was provided an upside-down view of a wide woman in a black dress who bullied her way across the floor, though not a single person stood in her way. Lina suspected that the queen was the type of person who would persecute air for being too breathable.

The monarch pushed her way to the forefront of the circle around Lina and her crew and stared at them, her left eye surveying the crew while her right stayed fixed on Lina.

"Good morning, Your Majesty," said Lina. "Allow me to introduce myself, I am Lina Tum-bel, ambassador of the Interplanetary Alliance."

The queen focused both eyes on Lina and bent over to inspect her more closely. She poked Lina with a long, slightly webbed finger. "Why are you hanging at this ridiculous height?"

"I had rather assumed it was a matter of advertisement," said Lina. The queen's eyes moved left and right, taking in the view. Then she snorted.

"I've known them all since they were born. Trust me, there is not much to advertise." She stood up. "You"—she pointed at the guard closest to Lina—"put them at an appropriate level." The guard pushed a button on the controls, elevating Lina up to the queen's face level.

"Thanks," said Lina. She turned to the guard. "Thanks." He was startled into nodding. "Now, as I was attempting to say before we were attacked, we're from Earth, and we are on a mission of peace to reconnect with you, our long-lost cousins."

The queen snorted again. "We're not lost. You're the ones who went dark."

Lina had the feeling blunt speech was the queen's preferred way to communicate, so she tried a different tack. "Well, yes, but now that we've recovered from our few centuries of insanity, we thought we'd pop by and say hello."

"Just hello? Nothing along the lines of rebuilding the nutrient pipeline?"

"That idea has been floated in some circles," admitted Lina. The Nebula Six bases and nearby planets had previously supplied water and a vast array of minerals and elements, all of which were crucial to rebuilding the Alliance.

"I'm sure it has. We can talk about it, but the To'Anda will want competitive market incentives."

"I would be more than happy to discuss terms," said Lina. "But perhaps we could discuss them in a more upright position?"

"I suppose." The queen gestured to the guard again.

He let them all down with a rapid descent and hard drop at the end. It was difficult to come out of that looking dignified, but Lina attempted to rally.

"Right," she said, standing as quickly as possible and stepping forward. The rush of blood from her head left her light-headed, and she stumbled as she stepped down from the platform. A quick movement by the guard saved her from a face-plant, and she found herself clinging to his arm and staring at him with blurred vision. Had his eyeball just done something weird? More weird than the usual weird? Something digital? Lina realized she was staring and pulled herself together.

Once right side up, she realized that, while the men were more or less the usual height, she was significantly shorter than the To'Andan woman. She could tell the queen was used to intimidating others with her size, but Lina's family all used the same trick, and if it didn't work over who got to shower first, it wasn't going to work here.

"Well," said Lina, smiling, "hello, so nice to see you from this angle."

"Why didn't you just rotate your eyes?" asked the prince, inspecting her from a distance she considered rather too close.

"Ah," said Lina, not backing up. "Interesting thought. But I'm afraid our eyes don't do that."

"Deficient," said the queen.

"Most likely," agreed Lina. "But we do make up for it by being able to turn our heads." She demonstrated neck movement.

"That makes your spinal column too easy to damage," said the cousin. "Also, it's weird-looking."

The queen reached out and slapped the back of his head. "Don't be rude to our guest. It's not her fault she's unfortunate-looking. Now then, Ambassador, if you would care to accompany me, we can discuss matters."

"My crew?" asked Lina.

"Will stay here," said the queen. She gestured to the guard, who nudged Lina forward. Lina glanced back at her crew. At least she'd gotten them right side up. Now all she had to do was get them out of this alive.

Chapter 2:

THE SPY CONSIDERS HIS OPTIONS

Sparrow Pandion had heard tales of Earth and the Interplanetary Alliance his entire life, but it had never crossed his mind that Terrans could be funny. In childhood legends, they were always heroes who strode across the stars like giants, remaking the galaxy in their image. He hadn't realized that a Terran could also be a charming woman with a wicked sense of humor that, at the moment, seemed to be sailing right over the heads of the assembled To'Andan court.

Of course, if you'd asked the childhood version of him if he'd ever turn out to be a spy, buried under a prosthetic mask and trailing behind a crown prince and his entourage, the answer would have also been a resounding *no*. Apparently, his child-self had lacked imagination.

The queen, all six foot eight of her, was pushing the ambassador on the subject of military assistance. Sparrow held his breath as the ambassador danced around the topic. Sparrow knew very well what Maarta wanted military assistance for: to crush his people. If she managed an alliance with Earth all of the plans, and all of the lives, of the Ránfuglar would be in jeopardy.

Queen Maarta was used to getting her way. She was intimidating in size and personality, and had been raised in the firm belief that getting her way was the natural order. Sparrow had watched her eat older, experienced stateswomen for breakfast. But the Terran ambassador was proving to be difficult. She was sitting in her seat, hands loosely clasped in her lap. She did not seem in the least bit agitated, despite the fact that the queen had hinted more than once that her life, and certainly the lives of her crew, might depend on affirmative answers. But the ambassador had yet to roll over on anything. She hadn't disagreed much, either, but she was refusing to say *yes*. It was an impressive display of political wrestling, and the queen was getting annoyed. Maarta was not an endurance athlete.

"That is enough. Earth will do what we want when their interests are our interests."

"I beg your pardon?" asked the ambassador.

Lina Tum-bel. He rolled the name over in his head. He liked it. She was medium height, with black hair and copper-colored eyes, and didn't look as if she had experienced any of the enhancements of the other humans in the nebula.

Like everyone else, the Ránfuglar had given up on expecting the return of Terrans or the Interplanetary Alliance. But now, faced with their presence, Sparrow realized they could change the entire political landscape in one move. Queen Maarta had clearly come to the same conclusion and was not about to let the chance to secure their assistance slip away.

"You will marry my son. Once Terran genes are here, they will act to protect their own interests.

The ambassador looked startled but thoughtful. "Well," she said, "that is certainly an interesting proposition, but I don't think that will have the effect you're looking for. Also, I rather think I will have to decline on the basis that I don't want to."

"It's decided," said the queen standing up, as if the ambassador hadn't spoken. "You." She pointed to Sparrow. "Go find my son. Give him the good news."

Sparrow bowed and left the room. This was not good news for anyone. Having the To'Andan align with Earth would be a disaster for his people. He needed to stop this wedding before the queen got what she needed to destroy the Ránfuglar. He thought he could get the ambassador off the base. The question was—would she trust him? And could he trust her?

Chapter 3:

THE AMBASSADOR DISCUSSES MATTERS WITH HER FIANCÉ

Far out in the stream grew a number of water-lilies, with broad green leaves, which seemed to float on the top of the water. The largest of these leaves appeared farther off than the rest, and the old toad swam out to it with the walnut-shell, in which little Thumbelina lay still asleep. The tiny little creature woke very early in the morning, and began to cry bitterly when she found where she was, for she could see nothing but water on every side of the large green leaf, and no way of reaching the land. Meanwhile the old toad was very busy under the marsh, decking her room with rushes and wild yellow flowers, to make it look pretty for her new daughter-in-law. Then she swam out with her ugly son to the leaf on which she had placed poor little Thumbelina. She wanted to fetch the pretty bed, that she might put it in the bridal chamber to be ready for her. The old toad bowed low to her in the water, and said, "Here is my son, he will be your husband, and you will live happily in the marsh by the stream."

Hans Christian Andersen, Thumbelina

Lina looked around her suite of rooms. The queen had been very pleased to point out the view, right before she'd walked out and the door had locked. Lina tapped a few buttons on her bracelet and scanned the room for listening devices. Everything came back clean. She hit the coms and contacted Captain Carbanado.

"Ambassador, it's good to hear from you. We were worried."

"I'm unharmed," said Lina. "What's your status?"

"There's a dampening field around the *Tempest*, blocking communications. We're using Teller's marks to get rudimentary messages through. They believe they can break free of the docking clamps. If we can get to the ship, then we can be out of here in two shakes of an Irishman's hand."

"Slight problem with that," said Lina. "It appears the queen would like me to marry her son."

There was a pause on the coms. "I'm sorry, did you say she wants you to marry her son?"

"Yes."

"The idiot with the frog for a face?"

"That's an inappropriate remark about potential allies, but yes."

"What the hell for?"

"Since leaving Earth, they've moved to a constitutional monarchy as a governing system. And like all monarchies, they believe that bloodlines strengthen political alliances. In other words, she wants a stronger tie with Earth, and she thinks if I have some toad—I mean To'Andan—babies, she's got a stronger shot at getting what she wants. Which is not an entirely unreasonable theory, just entirely unreasonable vis-a-vis myself."

"All right, but what does she want?"

"She wants to harvest the atmosphere of the planet—XJK56—with the small caveat that the Ránfuglar people are standing in the way. So she's hoping that if Earth sends troops she'll have the strength of numbers to claim the planet and rule the nebula with an iron web, er, fist."

"Who are the Ránfuglar?" asked the captain. "Our records only show one uninhabitable planet and two asteroid-based colonies in this nebula. The Toaran Station ran gases, ice, and water. The Morlina Station ran rock and minerals. Where did these Ránfuglar people come from?"

"No clue, but I can tell you that she's not letting me in on every facet of the political situation, and I have no intention of promising Earth's involvement in an internal conflict. Also, I have no intention of marrying the prince. So we need to get an escape plan in motion before I end up crown princess of To'Anda."

"Are you sure you don't want to rule your own mini-empire?" asked Carbanado, chuckling. The captain was a tall man of African descent, with soulful brown eyes and a booming laugh. He had been doubtful when she'd first come aboard, but five years later, they had developed a solid base of trust and affection. She knew she could rely on him.

"I'd have to assassinate the queen, and she looks difficult to kill. And then, frankly, staring at my husband over breakfast would be a bit of a problem, so I don't think so," said Lina. "How long do you need to make something happen?"

"Couple of hours," said Carbanado. "Edna thinks she can pry up the deck plating, destroy the platform tether, and float the platform up to the *Tempest*. Not so sure about coming to get you, though."

"I'll make my own way down to you," said Lina. "The queen is sending seamstresses to measure me for my wedding dress. Once I get rid of them, I'll see about getting down there."

"Good luck," said the captain.

"You too," she replied and tapped off.

She looked around the room speculatively. It was one thing to promise the captain that she could make it down to the hangar deck on her own; it was quite another to deliver. The suite was composed of a bedroom, a living area, and a generous—by space-based standards—bathroom. The living area opened onto a balcony through four double-glass doors framed by swoops of colorful fabric tied back with dramatic gold ropes, swagged as though she were entering a theater. She stepped out onto the balcony and took in a view of cascading smaller housing units that tumbled down to the edge of the bubble that encompassed the main portion of the base. Through meters-thick glass she could see the smaller To'Andan bases floating gently against the colorful miasma of the nebula and occasionally, through the haze of space gas, the distant stars twinkling kindly at her.

Somewhere on the other side of the nebula was a planet Terran maps designated as XJK-56. It had been deemed a dead planet with minimal atmosphere at the time of the initial survey. Lina found it odd that the queen would want to strip its atmosphere when the nebula was obviously still producing copious amounts of hydrogen, helium, and other gases. What did the planet have that the rest of the nebula couldn't produce?

Tearing her eyes from the view, she looked around again. Another balcony, presumably leading into another guest suite, was to her right. It was too far to jump, but if she had some sort of rope she might be able to lasso the decorative corner pillar and swing over. While she was contemplating her possible exit strategies, there was knock on the door.

Lina contemplated how best to deal with this. She knew very well the door was locked. She had no ability to open it to guests, even if she had wanted to.

"Come in," she said, settling herself onto the couch as if she had been comfortably relaxing.

The prince stepped into the room and then carefully closed the door behind him. He eyed her and tugged at the boatneck collar of his shirt. She waited for him to speak. He didn't appear to know what to say. She took a breath and tried to read him. He was a ball of static in her brain. Worry was his primary emotion.

"Your mother wishes us to be married," she said, looking for a conversation opener.

His worry spiked and she dropped the psychic connection. He was making her break out in a sweat.

"You don't really want to marry me, do you?" he asked nervously.

"Not particularly," she said.

"Do you think you could tell her that?"

"I did tell her that," said Lina. He looked crestfallen.

"That's all there is to it, then," he said, dejectedly dropping into a wing chair. He stared at the floor in misery. "We could probably use the lab to procreate, if you want. No reason to do it the old-fashioned way."

Lina wasn't sure how devastatingly insulted she should be. She had no intention of procreating with him in any fashion, so it shouldn't matter, but at minimum it felt like a very thoughtless comment.

"I mean, Mum's determined to get the job done, but she never cares *how* it gets done."

The prince appeared to have the social acumen of a fruit fly.

"Yes, I got that impression from her," said Lina. Her impression of the queen had been that she probably would get along quite well with Lina's mother. They both seemed to think that nerves and squeamishness were for other people.

The prince looked relieved.

"I expect it won't be so bad to be a parent," he said reflectively. "Everyone swears it's the absolute best, and if we don't like the offspring, then we'll just make Mum do all the work, since it was her idea to begin with."

"That's very practical," said Lina.

He made the patting hand gesture that seemed to be the To'Andan equivalent of a nod. "Mum always says I'm not to be creative. I just wish it didn't have to be so soon. I was going to the theater tonight. They've got a very good play going right now about a man who dresses up as a woman to become a politician and ends up falling in love with the prime minister."

"What do you mean, *so soon*?" asked Lina, leaning forward.

"She wants to do the thing tonight," said the prince, one of his eyes rolling up toward her.

"What? How can she possibly . . . She can't possibly arrange a wedding in a few hours!"

"She's the queen," said the prince with a shrug.

Lina took a deep breath, preparing to say something probably not appropriate for the prince's childlike mind, when the door opened and a contingent of seamstresses entered.

The prince eyed them with disfavor. "Maybe if I go now, I can catch a matinee. See you later."

The seamstresses giggled as if they had overheard some charming romantic banter and swarmed Lina, measuring her with scanning devices, as the prince made a hasty exit. Lina looked longingly toward the balcony. She should have taken her chances earlier and jumped.

Chapter 4:

THE AMBASSADOR MAKES A HASTY EXIT

Three hours later, Lina was fully sealed and buttoned into an enormous white wedding dress. It had acres of train and a high, pointed collar that—Lina suspected—was intended to hide the fact that she had a neck. The underdress was an emerald green and felt slightly oily, as if the fabric wasn't natural. The dresser, when questioned, pointed out what should have been obvious: there were virtually no organic fabrics or fibers on an asteroid base. Everything was created from the chemicals and gases the To'Andan harvested from the nebula. The overdress was weighed down with embroidery, crystals, and drapes of chains. It hampered her movements further with long, stiff sleeves and a tight bodice with a row of tiny buttons that compressed her cleavage upward to an impressive degree. The dress itself probably weighed twenty pounds. Her old clothes, of course, had disappeared in the process of her changing.

"The next person to take this dress off will be your husband," said the dresser cheerfully, finishing the buttons and patting the bell of the skirt affectionately, as if it were a dog.

"Mm," said Lina, as if that were an actual comment. She waited until the door closed and then hit her com bracelet.

"Carbanado, what's your status?"

"We're almost through the platform. Edna needs a few more minutes to blow the tether. Now would be a good time make a polite exit."

"On my way," said Lina. She gathered up yards' worth of train, pulled it through her legs, wrapped it around her waist, and tied it. She was now wearing enormous bloused diaper pants. The effect was ridiculous, but it made maneuvering more possible.

She pulled the drape tie-backs off the wall, tied them together, and went out to the balcony. Working quickly, she threw the drape cords, looping them around the finial of the balcony across from her. She tested weight on it and then allowed herself to swing out into the empty space. She enjoyed the split second of swinging freedom, then began the arduous task of climbing the rope. Hauling twenty extra pounds of dress made for an interesting experience. She was sweating by the time she got one hand on the balcony edge. She was fumbling, trying to get her other hand over without ending up dangling by her fingertips, when another hand reached down and began to pull her up.

"I was coming to get you," said a pleasant male voice, "but I guess this will work too."

She realized as she climbed past his codpiece that it was her guard from earlier in the day—the only person in the room who had found her funny.

"And was there a particular reason you were coming to get me?" she asked, perching on the balustrade. He hadn't made any aggressive moves, but gentlemen who called unexpectedly weren't always to be trusted.

"I was thinking about taking in the sights elsewhere. I thought you might be interested in making a similar trip."

Lina considered her options. Having a local guide would certainly make for a speedier exit. She extended her thoughts and attempted to *read* him. There was excitement, a hint of nerves, and a little bit of worry. She chased the worry, trying to find the cause. The only thing that came to the front was a matter of trust. Could he trust her?

One of the most natural of reactions was to think that of course she could be trusted—she was she, and the hero of the story. But one of the first lessons of the Ambassadorial Corps was that in reality the answer was frequently *no*. The mission had to take priority, and sometimes that meant little people got lost in the big objective. Having watched her mother make the big decisions time and time again, she was no stranger to the concept, but it had always been her personal goal as an ambassador to make her word mean something. She tried never to promise anything she couldn't deliver. She didn't know what this To'Andan wanted, but if he could help her, then she would do her best to help him. She hoped that would be enough.

"I could use a little vacation," she said. "Can you get us to the hangar bay? My crew is prepping to leave."

He nodded, an awkward gesture on the To'Andan, and she realized that he was the only one she'd seen attempt it.

"Lead the way, then," she said.

The guard led her through the suite and into the service corridors. Unlike the guest quarters and open spaces of the base, the back passageways were cramped, narrow, and color coded, with steep narrow stairs and the metallic tang of poorly recycled air. They felt familiar to Lina—as if she had returned to any of the hundred ships on which she'd grown up. The To'Andan braced his arms on the railings of a particularly steep set of stairs and slid down. Lina was just behind him and did the same. She thought his body registered surprise as he turned back to assist her, but his face was once again expressionless.

There was a beep in her right ear and she tapped her bracelet to pick up the call. "You might want to be here soon," said Carbanado. "We've got a bit of traffic down here, and it could get messy."

"Working on it," said Lina. The guard glanced back. "We need to pick up the pace."

He nodded and began to jog. They wound their way through the maze of back hallways and rounded a corner. She saw him hesitate and looked around his broad shoulders to see a cluster of To'Andan blocking an intersection.

"No time to double back," she heard the guard mutter. He began to reach for the stick weapon he wore at his side.

"OK, well, they'll just have to move," she said. She shoved him forward, filled her lungs, and tried to remember what her mother sounded like in these situations. "Make a hole!" she yelled.

The To'Andan scattered instantly or flattened themselves against the wall. Lina and the guard sprinted down the hallway and turned a corner, all the while expecting to hear angry shouts.

He paused at a junction, seeming to hesitate over directions, and Lina looked back. As yet, there were no pursuers or shouts of outrage.

"They really bought that," said Lina, surprised.

"Breasts count for a lot here," he said, selecting the red hallway. "They probably assumed you knew what you were doing."

"What a charming idea," said Lina.

The guard chuckled but kept moving. They reached a door and he stopped, holding up his hand for her to do the same. He peered around the door and then stepped through, looked both ways, and beckoned her. Ahead of them she could see the brighter, open space of the hangar deck.

There was a yell from behind them, and a klaxon horn began to sound. The hallway filled with flashing lights.

"Run," said the guard, reaching for his weapon.

Lina did as she was told, sprinting for the hangar bay. Ahead of her, three To'Andan stepped into the hallway, blocking her progress. Through the opening, she could see Carbanado and Fina battling to hold position on the floating platform. Edna was ripping plates and wires off the platform, and as Lina watched, the hangar bay doors high above the floor began the arduous process of closing.

Lina focused on her more immediate problem. One of the guards was stepping forward, his stick telescoping out to full length, readying for a fight.

Lina pulled up short and brushed the dust off her dress. "Gentlemen, I'm so glad you're here. I have been attacked. I need your help in subduing those rebels."

They hesitated, eyeing the guard behind her who was now battling their friends. This allowed her to approach and get close enough to run an illusion. It was a minor infraction, but she didn't see any other options. She grabbed the gun from his belt and pointed at the melee behind her. "Help him!" she commanded, pushing hard on their rescue imperative.

Her guard looked around in confusion as the three launched

themselves into attack on his behalf. She beckoned and he came running.

They ran into the hangar bay. She was stumbling, trying to move and concentrate on holding the illusion at the same time. She wasn't good enough to do both.

"Hey!" the guard yelled, grabbing her arm as she veered dangerously close to an open shaft. The illusion snapped and she blinked up at him, trying to remember where she was.

"Right," she said. She turned and fired at the door lock. The doors began to close. Across the hangar bay, there was an explosion. The To'Andan fell back and the floating platform began to rise, Carbanado and Fina clinging to the edge as it rose toward the *Tempest*. In response, the ship fired up its thrusters, and they all heard the creak of docking clamps straining to hold the craft.

Carbanado and Fina regained the platform surface, and she could see them all looking down at her.

"I have another way off the base," said the guard. "But we'll need a distraction. Can they blow the F2 boiler once they're out?"

Lina tapped her com. "Captain, I've got another exit option. Once you're out, blow the F2 boiler and meet at the rally point."

"Aye, Ambassador," said Carbanado, and she saw him throw a salute from the platform. She saluted back and looked to her To'Andan.

"This way," he said. They ran across the hangar bay, and Lina had the thought she always did when running for her life: the Ambassadorial Corps should add more physical fitness to their requirements. Behind them she heard the cannons of the *Tempest* fire. Probably attempting to halt the closing of the hangar bay doors.

Her guard led the way through a maze of back tunnels and then finally into a darkened corridor. He paused at a panel, ripping it off the wall and pulling out data chips and wiring with abandon. Lina leaned against the wall, panting. Her dress had come undone and was trailing behind her. She gathered it up as the guard moved on to a second panel. The was a loud boom from somewhere below them.

"They've hit the boiler," said the guard. "Not much time." He worked faster, and then a piece of the wall fell away. He grabbed Lina by the arm and pushed her through as an explosion from below flexed the decking beneath their feet and threw her to the floor.

Chapter 5:

THE AMBASSADOR LEARNS HOW TO TAKE OFF CLOTHES

The To'Andan guard stepped through the opening and slammed a door closed behind him. She heard the distinct hiss and clunk of docking seals disengaging.

She looked around the room and realized she was in the main hull of a small craft. Her immediate surroundings were the living quarters. Forward through a door was a cockpit; to her right a small bathroom and another door that was closed and had the double safety seals she associated with fireproof doors. She guessed that was the engine room.

She attempted to struggle to her feet, but the dress was now twined around her legs. The To'Andan guard stepped over her and hurried to the cockpit.

She had just managed to regain her feet and had taken two steps to the center of the room when her dress snagged on a chair. She pitched forward and put her hands out to catch herself, only to find that she was no longer falling. The gravity had switched off, and she bobbed in the center of the room like a balloon on a string. Through the window of the cockpit she could see the To'Andan base drifting farther and farther away, a massive fire burning on one sub-level. The *Tempest* was speeding away, trailing a comet's tail of pursuing ships. There was a quiet hiss as the To'Andan skillfully applied the barest hint of thrusters, spinning the ship and pointing it in the opposite direction. Moments later, windows port and starboard were uncovered as solar sails unfurled and locked into position.

This was all fascinating. She had only seen solar-sail ships in a museum, and she was anxious to get a closer look. She tried to spin and catch hold of her train to pull it free, but the stiff collars blocked her view and she couldn't see where to grab. After a few moments of frustration, she looked down to realize the To'Andan had exited the cockpit and was standing firmly on the floor. His expression remained impassive as ever, but her telepathic senses suggested that he was laughing at her.

"Magnetic boots?" she asked.

"Yes. Sorry, I don't want to turn on anything but life support until we're well away. I'll help you down as soon as I change."

Lina thought that was a bit rude. Surely changing clothes could wait until—

Lina's thoughts stopped as the man reached up, seized his eyebrow, and tore off a chunk of flesh.

"Ah! Chunks!" She spun away, covering her eyes with her hand. "I'm sorry," she babbled. "That was culturally insensitive. If you want to tear your face off, you should feel free. I just really have a thing about chunks."

Much to her mother's chagrin. It was why she had washed out of the military. Even in simulation, the tendency of flesh to explode into thick meaty slabs when fired upon wasn't something she could ever get her head or stomach around. Her war-hero mother had called her a *delicate flower* and pointed her, dismissively, to the Ambassadorial Corps. Lina had tried to uphold the family name as best she could from there, but she always had the feeling Mother found her work a step down from even the most basic

Fight Grunt.

"All done," said the man, coming around to her side. "You can look."

She blinked down at the distinctly human, non-To'Andan face beneath her. He had stripped off his helmet and armor as well and was down to his skin. His arms were still the To'Andan greenish-gray, but his skin from the waist up was pale white. She glanced back at the helmet, armor, and conglomeration of rubbery face parts he had left floating above the table. "I knew your eyes didn't look right!"

He grinned. It was a good grin—dimple on one side, slightly lopsided. He had blue eyes and red-gold hair that was floating up from his scalp in fly-away wings. "The eyes are the hardest, but most people don't look that closely."

He clicked his heels together, releasing the magnetic hold, and floated up to look her in the eye. They stared at each other, and she restrained herself from reaching into his mind to find out what he thought of her.

"My name's Sparrow," he said, bobbing slightly against the ceiling.

"Like the bird?" she asked, feeling pleased with the name in an indefinable way.

"What is a bird?" he asked. His expression intensified into curiosity, and she could tell he meant the question honestly.

Instinctively, she held up her hands, cupping them as if holding the goldfinch that had been in her grandmother's house. "It's a . . ." She hesitated, then spread her hands to let her imaginary bird go. How was she supposed to explain birds to someone who'd probably been born in space? "It's an animal that flies," she said, which she felt short-changed the entire bird species on a massive level.

"*Ránfuglar*," he said. She raised a questioning eyebrow, but he was looking down at the floor beneath their floating feet and didn't explain. "Yes," he said, looking up at her. "Like a bird."

"You must be Ránfuglar," she guessed. "A spy?" That would explain a lot about his motivation and his concern about trusting her.

He grinned again. "Yes. And we would like to have a chance to make our alliances with Earth first. Or at least inform you of some of the realities of what Maarta is proposing before you agree to it."

"Well, since I would like a chance to *not* be forced into marriage and reproduction, I think I'd be willing to at least talk." Talking was about all she could commit to at this point. Clearly, nebula politics were a bit complex.

"I thought you might feel that way."

She liked the way his eyes twinkled.

There was a beep from the cockpit and he pushed off the ceiling, transitioning back to the deck of the ship with an ease that spoke of practice.

"Gravity's coming back on shortly," he yelled back to her.

"I don't know," she said, surveying the room from her vantage point near the ceiling. "Maybe I like floating above everyone."

He came back into the common area and stared up at her, a smile hovering on his face. "But I'm the only everyone here."

"Maybe I like to feel tall for once." Her brother had always called her Tiny. It wasn't her fault that she wasn't a giant like the rest of the family. At least she didn't have to have her space suits custom made. But it was nice to have a chance to loom over someone—although Sparrow did not look as though he was feeling very loomed at.

There was a whoosh as the gravity came back on and dumped her unceremoniously floor-ward. He caught her easily, obviously having predicted where she would land, and set her gently on her feet.

"Can't help you with that," he said, now looking down at her. He wasn't as giant as her brother, but he certainly wasn't petite. "But how about a change of clothes?"

"I could not want that more," she said. "I only wish we had a torpedo tube to launch this dress out of."

He laughed as he opened a cabinet near the bathroom door. "Unfortunately, these are all my size," he said pulling out a pair of folded pants and a shirt. "I wasn't expecting guests."

"I will make do," she promised, reaching for the clothes.

"I'll help you get out of the dress," he said, reaching for the buttons on the front.

"I think I can manage," she said, stepping back. His tone hadn't been sexual, so perhaps that was a common offer where he was from, but Lina wasn't comfortable with having strangers help her out of her clothes. The To'Andan helping her into the dress had been bad enough. Sparrow seemed on the point of saying something, but then shrugged.

"All right, I'll be in the cockpit." He grabbed a packet of something from the same cupboard as the clothes and went forward, politely shutting the door between the rooms.

Lina set down the clothes. First she freed her train from where it had been hung up on a chair, and then she kicked off her shoes. Last she reached up and tugged at the first button on the dress.

It didn't budge.

She pulled harder. The results were the same. She tried other buttons. Still nothing. She marched into the kitchen, pulled a knife from the magnetic strip above the sink, and sawed carefully at a button. The button severed and almost fell—and then, as she watched, a thread of the dress reached out and pulled it back on.

She swore at the button and sawed it off again, plus two more. The dress put them back on. In frustration, she attempted to yank the dress off over her head, but it was cinched tight to her waist, and the harder she pulled, the tighter it seemed to go. She concluded a string of swear words and sat down, breathing heavily, and tried to think through the problem. After a moment, she stood up and went to the cockpit door.

"Sparrow?" she called, knocking on the door. It slid open. He was leaning against the console—not even pretending to fly—as if he'd been waiting for her. He'd also been scrubbing off the gray-green To'Andan skin color. He was now only greenish around his elbows and wrists.

"Want some help now?"

"If there was a problem with the dress, why didn't you just tell me?"

"You sounded so confident," he said, with a shrug.

"Well, I should sound confident. I have never previously had a problem taking off my own clothes."

"I meant, how was I to know you didn't have some way to take it off? You're from Earth—presumably you know things I don't."

"Well, you're from Ránfuglar, so presumably you know more about local problems! Or perhaps you just like to listen to me swear at buttons?"

"Those were some good swear words," he said. "I definitely learned some new ones."

"Are you going to help or not?" demanded Lina.

"Yes," he said with another grin. He came out into the living quarters, and she backed the parade float of a dress into the center of the floor, waiting for him to perform some magic.

"OK," she said. "What's the trick?"

"No trick," he said, shaking his head. "It's easy." He reached out and began to unbutton the dress. Under his hands, the fabric parted easily. She gaped at him. He laughed. "It's a To'Andan wedding dress. It will only open for a male."

Lina thought that one through. "That doesn't work. What happens when two girls get married?"

He shook his head, still unbuttoning the string of tiny buttons. "Only women and men marry in To'Andan society."

"What?" Lina didn't believe it. "That's statistically impossible. Every society has homosexual relationships."

"Relationships, yes. Marriages, no. Children always belong to their mother, but the men only have rights to the offspring if they get married. There isn't a reason for two women to marry because they would obviously own their own children."

"But wouldn't it be a problem if someone's partner died and

left children?"

"In the case of death, the children always go to the mother's family, marriage or no marriage. But men would only get visitation rights if they had a marriage. And if two men want to have children, then one of them has to change sex. To'Andan are born asexual, so switching is a fairly easy transition for them if they get the right hormone dose. They say in times of stress or lacking the appropriate number of females, some will even change on their own."

"They must have used amphibian genes, I suppose. But hang on, it's a matriarchal society," protested Lina. "Wouldn't that mean someone ends up with a better social standing? How do they decide who gets the short end of the stick?"

He shrugged and finished the last button. "That was outside the scope of my inquiries."

"Huh," she said, considering To'Andan marital arrangements. "What now?" she asked, looking down at the green underdress. The thin seam the seamstress had used to fasten her into the dress was no longer visible. She had no idea where to even direct Sparrow to try to open it. He appeared to be untroubled and, instead of answering her, leaned into her breasts and exhaled along the entire length of her torso. Lina let out a startled yip and clutched the underdress as it parted under his breath. "A little warning!"

"Sorry," he said, although he didn't look excessively sorry. "Didn't think it would open that fast. You should be able to take it from here."

He disappeared back into the cockpit, and Lina took a deep breath. She didn't think she was overly prudish, but she really did draw the line at having strange men breathe on her breasts. No matter how cute they were.

PART II:

Of Escapes, Close Calls & Beetles

So the leaf swam away with her farther and farther, till it brought her to other lands. A graceful little white butterfly constantly fluttered round her, and at last alighted on the leaf. Thumbelina pleased him, and she was glad of it, for now the toad could not possibly reach her, and the country through which she sailed was beautiful, and the sun shone upon the water, till it glittered like liquid gold.

Hans Christian Andersen, Thumbelina

Chapter 6:

THE AMBASSADOR LEARNS MORE ABOUT HER COMPANION

Sparrow's clothes were more of the To'Andan plasticine fabrics, and Lina spared a thought to miss the small luxuries of hemp and cotton. She wasn't particularly fond of her ambassadorial outfits, which she found boring, but she missed her bra a good deal. It had disappeared when she'd been strapped into the wedding gown.

She ducked into the bathroom to scrub the To'Andan make-up off her face. One look was enough to convince her that Sparrow's offer of assistance in dress removal had definitely not been sexual. They had painted her mouth a bright garish red that doubled the size of her already rather large lips. They had also used a trowel to put eyeshadow in green with dark liner that seemed to mimic the To'Andan eye circles. They had then braided her black hair so that it stood up in a crest along her head, and added crystals to the shaved side. Her face looked ridiculous, but she rather liked the hair. She'd have to remember the look the next time she wanted something fancier. She scrubbed her face, unwound her hair, and finished changing. She thought about putting her hair back into a braid but decided she didn't want to take the time and went into the cockpit.

"What's the range on this ship's communications array?" she asked as she entered. "I was hoping to get a message off to my ship."

"What communications array?" he replied drily. He pointed

to a small display on the dash and she realized the level of technology she was dealing with.

"Okaaaay." She pulled off her bracelet, flattened it out, and set it to pair with the ship.

He was moving about the cabin adjusting various controls and periodically consulting a display card, flipping through various diagrams. It looked like the ship's manual. She hoped he knew what he was doing.

"You said you had a rendezvous point with your ship. Will they meet us there even if you don't contact them?"

"Yes. They should. But—"

"Right," he agreed with a nod. "What are the coordinates?"

She displayed the coordinates and he manually added them to the ship's navigation. The ship really was a museum piece. "How long do you think it will take us to get there?"

"Approximately eighty-four to ninety hours," he said, looking faintly embarrassed.

"About four days. OK," said Lina, absorbing the fact that she would be spending four days in confined quarters with a handsome stranger who apparently felt no need to put a shirt on and had breathed on her boobs.

"This wasn't supposed to be a speedy escape route."

The bracelet beeped and she checked the analysis. Her options were limited. She settled for a recorded and encoded message. It was practically the equivalent of a message in a bottle, but it would have to do.

"Exit successful. Rendezvous in about ninety hours."

She hit Send and sat down in the copilot's chair.

"It's possible that we'll be earlier," he offered. "I may be able to do a few things to speed it up."

She shrugged and stared out the window at the shifting clouds of gas. "Earlier is a pleasant surprise. Later makes them worry."

She stood up and leaned on the console, trying to get a better view upward and out into the nebula. The colors were indescribable, and the eddies of gas made the view like watching a kaleidoscope. She had never seen anything like it. She thought of her family, her clan, and everyone she had left behind on Earth. When she'd left, she hadn't been sure it was the right decision, but she had seen a lot of amazing things since then. And nothing at all like the nebula. She laughed suddenly, and Sparrow looked up from the controls in surprise.

"Something funny?"

"I was just thinking of the day I told my brother I'd been selected to be an ambassador. He told me I would be wasting my life on cocktail parties and contract negotiations."

Sparrow snorted. "Last time I saw my brother, he told me that I should stop playing dress-up and come home."

"Brothers: can't live with them, and Mom won't let you kill them."

He chuckled. "So true. Although I suspect they feel the same about us. Do you have a lot of siblings?"

"Just Tommy and I," she replied. "What about you?"

"I'm the youngest of three. One sister, one brother."

"Ah, well, the youngest is always the cleverest."

He looked amused. "I like the idea, but I have my doubts about that from time to time."

"So do I," she said. "Usually when I'm fleeing for my life. But I certainly will not be telling that to Tommy anytime soon."

"I said I might not be the cleverest, not that I was *hálfviti*."

"*Hálfviti?*"

"Uh . . . like really stupid? Idiot, maybe? It's the settler's language. Not many people speak it anymore, but there are still some words we can't seem to leave behind."

She laughed, dropped back into her chair, and stared out the window. Maybe four days would be all right. He certainly didn't look bad shirtless, and he had a sense of humor. And it would give her the opportunity to find out more about the politics of the region.

They sailed on in silence for a few more minutes. He was, at last, actually sitting in the pilot's chair, seeming close to completing his checklists. Finally, he sat back and turned to her.

"Hungry?" In response, her stomach growled loudly. "I'll take that as a yes. Let's see what got packed in the galley."

She followed him into the living area, where he grabbed another shirt from the cupboard. She was mildly disappointed— she'd just accustomed herself to the idea of enjoying naked man chest for four days. As he pulled on the shirt, she caught a glimpse of two massive scars running across his shoulder blades and down his back. Perhaps Earth wasn't the only place with violent stories to tell.

"All right," he said digging into the pantry. "We have boring." He pulled out a block of food cubes. "More boring." Food cubes of a different flavor. "A gift from Mama." His intonation of *mama* was strange, as if he was pronouncing it from a different language. As she pondered his linguistics, she saw that he had placed a bar of something that looked very much like chocolate on the table. Lina heard herself inhale greedily. He glanced up with a grin. "And a gift from Finch—my sister." He put a bottle of clear liquid down on the table.

"Are you all named after birds?" she asked, momentarily distracted from the chocolate.

"I have no idea, since until I met you, I hadn't been able to figure out what birds were. There are a few references to them in the archives, but nothing explicit. It's like everyone just assumed they didn't need explanation. My brother is Tanager."

Lina nodded. "Also a species of bird. I wish I had access to the library. I'd show you pictures."

"They're all family names," he said with a shrug. He set about dividing the food cubes onto plates and then poured small glasses of liquid from the bottle. Lina took a seat, letting him arrange dinner in front of her. She could feel herself getting tired while she sat. It had been a very long day. She wondered if she could politely just go to bed after dinner. She took a cautious sip of her drink. It was peppery but very slightly sweet, and the burn down her throat was a slow build. It was the kind of thing that would buy her a ton of favors in the fleet. She wondered if she could somehow end up with a few cases by the end of this. She looked up and realized Sparrow was watching her.

"Yes? No?" he asked, putting her plate down in front of her. There was a delicate square of chocolate on the corner.

"Yes," she said. "If you can produce that in quantity, you'll make mass credits off the grunts in the fleet."

He slathered his food cube in some sort of sauce and seemed to consider the idea. "It would depend," he said after a moment. "Expanding a particular crop always has to be balanced with the needs of the population. Credits might not be to our advantage if we can't feed our people."

Lina took another sip. "It's an organic product? Not chemically synthesized?"

"It's from a type of pepper—diarvins. It's called diecohol."

Lina considered the ramifications of his statements. Growing crops in space wasn't impossible, but the fact that they were growing on a scale to feed a population of any size was impressive. She absentmindedly ate the food cubes, which was the best way to eat food cubes, and tried to think about what she wanted to ask Sparrow and how not to sound like she was interrogating him.

"Can I ask—" He stopped, blushing slightly.

"What?" Instinctively, she reached out for a *reading*. Curiosity and low-level excitement pinged off him like sparks. She liked his brain—it was fizzy, like champagne.

"I want to ask about Earth, but I'm afraid I'll sound like an idiot or too . . . political."

"And I want to ask about the Ránfuglar. So how about you ask, I'll ask. If we don't want to answer, then we have to pass our next turn."

He nodded. "Me first. What happened to Earth and the Alliance?"

"There was a civil war between a faction generally called Naturalists and a faction called Progressives. The Naturalists wanted to kill off a large portion of the population and return the Earth to a natural state. They don't believe in body modifications and are deeply suspicious of technology."

"Well, considering that you don't seem particularly upset by the To'Andan, I guess the Progressives won."

"Yes," said Lina. "Although in general the Ambassadorial Corps is known for our disconcertingly open minds, so you won't find many of us getting upset by . . . much. The strain of prejudice is still there, though. A lot of Progressives don't love the idea of modifications; they just didn't think the Naturalists should be allowed to go around killing people. Anyway, the war eventually involved all the closest planets and took down the Alliance. It's only been in the last hundred years or so that we've been able to put things back together and reach back out. It's a bit amusing to find that by trying to reclaim Earth the Naturalists seem to have pushed most of the rest of the galaxy into some form of modification. Humans needed Earth in order to stay human."

"Huh," he said, sitting back in his chair.

"My turn," she said. "Who are the Ránfuglar? We have records of the bases that must have become the To'Andan and the . . . Moliter—did I get that right?" He nodded. "But who are the Ránfuglar?"

"After the Alliance trade route collapsed and became too dangerous, everyone in the nebula had some tough choices to make. As you point out, unmodified humans don't make it very far out here alone. But not everyone was happy with the direction the modifications were going, or with the very idea of substantially changing who we are as humans. The Ránfuglar are the To'Andan and the Moliter who didn't want to be modified. We're the ones who left."

"OK, but where did you go?"

He grinned and shook his head. "That's two questions. It's my turn again."

"Who invented these stupid rules?" she said, taking another sip of the diecohol. It made her feel warm all over. "Fine. Bring it. I can give you so much political history you'll beg for mercy."

"I'm sure you can. How about this, though: what does the Alliance want in the nebula?"

Lina chewed some more food cube and thought about how to answer that.

"You're going to pass, aren't you?"

"No," she said, and took another drink. "I'm really not. But that's a complex question. The general goal of the Alliance is to rebuild what we had before the civil war."

She didn't add that one of the things pushing the expansion previously was population growth. War had taken care of that. Now the attention was more on rekindling the spark of innovation and pulling the human race back from the dark ages of war. The goal of her current mission was to get the trade routes rebuilt—to get resources flowing again. Bringing bases into the Alliance was the most likely way to make that happen, but it wasn't necessarily the goal. They didn't necessarily need more people hanging on the system. They needed planets that could contribute to growth. But it was hard to explain that without sounding rude.

"And what happens when someone says *no, thanks*?" he asked.

"That's two questions. My turn."

"Who made these rules?" he quoted and took a sip of his own drink.

"Where did the Ránfuglar go?"

"To the planet."

"It's not habitable," she said.

"No, it's not," he agreed. "But the Ránfuglar bases are built in the exosphere of the planet."

"So having the To'Andan strip off the atmosphere would be a serious problem?"

"That's two, but I'll answer it. Yes, for a good number of reasons, stripping the atmosphere would be catastrophic for us." His face was serious, and a quick *reading* indicated that he felt the urgent need to communicate his message to her.

She considered her meeting with the To'Andan queen. She had suspected that the queen had wanted Alliance help against the Ránfuglar, but this sounded like more than a territory grab. And from the urgency in Sparrow's mind, it felt more like genocide. She frowned.

"I don't understand. Why would the To'Andan want the planet? It's a virtually dead planet, according to the records. There wasn't much atmosphere to begin with. Why do the To'Andan care? There has to be something else they're getting out of it."

"And that's three. I'm going to want bonus questions."

She laughed. "Granted. Just explain." Lina took another sip of her drink as he began.

"After the fall of the Alliance, the nebula was divided up. Territories were created within it. No one wanted the planet, and when the Ránfuglar left, we bargained for it. Everyone was happy with what they got. What neither the To'Andan nor the Moliter realized was what we wanted to do with the planet. Namely, make it habitable."

"Terraforming was in its infancy back then. And you just said no one was living there."

"Not yet. But our current estimates put habitation at five hundred years away."

Lina sat back in her chair. "I saw the original planet scans. There is no way . . . You did that on your own?"

"My people did that. But now that we're getting closer, the To'Andan and the Moliter are no longer so happy about our deal."

"An entire planet of resources . . . Crop and population growth alone . . . It would change the balance of power in the nebula."

"Exactly," he said. "And the closer we get, the more they've tried to push us out. War is coming for our people, and our choices are speed up habitation, expand our war capabilities, or get allies. We've done what we could on the first two, but honestly, we could use allies."

Lina took a deep breath and another drink. This was a lot more than another space base to add the Alliance's charm bracelet. A new planet was exactly what they needed. And if the Ránfuglar could manage terraforming on their own in the armpit of the universe with no resources, what could they do with the entire back catalog of Earth's technology at their disposal?

"What do you think?" he asked, watching her carefully. "Is there room for us in the Alliance?"

"Yes," said Lina, honestly. "I mean, we'll have to negotiate, but we should be able to reach some sort of agreement. Space bases are nice, but they tend to only produce one product and they're difficult to maintain. A planet, on the other hand . . ."

"Everyone wants a planet," he said with a grin. He felt like champagne again, popping with relief. "All right, my turn," he said. "What does ground feel like?"

"Oh," she said, and took a hasty drink, finishing the glass. She could tell she was a little drunk, which was impressive off just one glass. But she thought she could manage a little buzz. Politics while drunk was practically day one of training in the Ambassadorial Corps. "Ask something else. Ask anything. The political system. The Voting Rights Act of 2542. Anything."

"I don't want to know about those things. I want to know what ground is. We have gardens, so I understand dirt. But the old texts always talk about different kinds of ground: fields and hills and beach. What's beach?"

She blinked, *reading* him. He really wanted to know.

"I'm sorry. That's the stuff I'm really bad at. I can tell you all sorts of facts and figures, but the stuff that matters, like oceans and sky and what it smells like after it rains . . . I mean, I tell people that birds are animals that fly." She couldn't believe she was admitting to this—usually she just tried to bluff her way through these kinds of questions. She felt flushed. Was the room getting warmer? Was she really *that* drunk?

"Aren't they?"

"Yes, but that is like saying the To'Andan are a people who are a little bit green. It's true, but it doesn't really get to the heart of the matter. I'm sorry, but you've managed to get stuck with the least poetic Terran around. Anything I say will sound . . . lame, and it deserves more."

"Oh. I did want to know what beach was," he said, the champagne bubbles dissipating. She was surprised to discover that he was sad, but he was setting the desire aside. The connection was still open between them, and she was struggling to shut down the reciprocal sadness she felt for him. It felt, in his head, like he was used to not getting what he wanted, and that felt more than a little bit crushing.

She was struck with an impulse. It was so wrong, but maybe . . . She glanced over her shoulder. She couldn't believe she was even thinking this.

She looked at him again and could feel the weight of sadness hanging over him, and suddenly she wanted to make him smile. She felt hot and flushed—and like the Earth's worst representative.

The world swam in front of her eyes a little. The sadness underneath the initial layer of thoughts seemed incredibly thick, but maybe she could make it a little better.

"I could . . . You want the beach?"

"Yes?" he said.

"You can't tell anyone," she said, and placed her hand on his face.

Chapter 7:

THE SPY DISCOVERS THE PROBLEMS OF INTERPLANETARY RELATIONS

She put her hand over his eyes, and then he was . . . somewhere else. Sparrow had an overwhelming sense of exposure and blinding light and crashing noise. His eyes adjusted slowly. There was nothing above him but a burning sun and an empty sky a shade of blue he had never seen. The heat of the sun was a palpable presence on his skin. There was a screech of anger above him, jerking his attention upward. Two small flying things battled angrily. Black. Crow. White. Gull. Knowledge filtered in as if from a distance. He gasped as his feet were covered suddenly in cold and wet. He looked down as frothy cold water receded from his legs, sucking hungrily at his toes. Wave. Ocean. Under his feet the . . . sand . . . shifted, leaving with the water.

He looked outward, identifying the loud crash and rush of noise as the action of the water pummeling the sand. Tide. The water frothed white at the tips before driving into the sand and sliding up to meet his feet again, then receded, leaving a dark dividing line. Beyond the waves was an expanse the color of emeralds. Or an impossible dark blue like the crystals in Moliter tunnel lights. He'd never seen so much unobstructed space. He pulled his gaze away from the sea and looked around. The sand continued in either direction as far as he could see. Behind him, a series of small grass-covered dunes blocked his view. The wind pushed against him, straightening the hair on his arm and lifting it from his head. He turned back to the sea and saw a sandpiper run by on stiff legs before spreading its wings and lifting into the sky. The movement was so painfully familiar and new to him all at the same time. The wind blew against him again, hitting him in the face with a mist of wetness that tasted salty and smelled of seaweed and fish and something sweet he couldn't identify. He looked around again, realizing where he was. This was the beach.

He blinked, and when he opened his eyes, he was standing in the living quarters of the *Ember*.

"Birds," he said, putting his hand up to his lips, where he could still taste the sea. "Those were birds."

He was overwhelmed with a sense of gratitude. He wasn't sure how she'd given him that moment, but it had been the most amazing moment of his life. He normally avoided touching other people, but he wanted to hug her. To touch her. To connect in some way. He took a step back toward the table, but it was as if his movement set off hers. She pushed away from the table looking pale and ill.

"What did I do?" Lina put her hands up to her face, horrified. She stumbled and clutched at the chair. She looked at her empty cup. "What did you do?" she gasped, staring at him.

"Nothing!" He could feel their easy camaraderie slipping away like sand under his feet. He stepped forward again and she flailed backward, obviously unstable and dizzy. He took another step and so did she, but this time she lost her balance and hit the floor.

He ran to her side. Her long hair, which he could only now compare to the blackness of a crow's wing, splashed across the floor. She seemed barely conscious, but she kept trying to push his hands off her. Her pulse was rapid and her skin was clammy. He yanked the med-kit out of its mounting on the wall and pressed the scanner to her arm.

"You drugged me," she slurred.

"No, I didn't!" He wasn't sure what had gone wrong. She'd only had one glass of the diecohol. It shouldn't have had this effect on anyone.

"Drugged me," she muttered again, and passed out.

The med-scanner beeped with the diagnosis: *biochemical interaction resulting in psychotropic side effects*.

Or maybe he had drugged her.

Fjandinn.

He flipped through an additional list of curse words, but went back to the first one. *Fjandinn.* He was in such deep *skít*.

He scrolled through the med-scanner prescription, which basically amounted to sleeping it off. Sparrow ran his hand through his hair. How had he managed to screw this up? They needed her and they needed Earth, and beyond that, he'd liked her. She was smart, funny, more than a little bit of a firebrand, and—not that it was relevant, but it still mattered—she had a truly great set of breasts. Now she was going to hate him, and Tanager was going to kill him.

Chapter 8:

THE AMBASSADOR FINDS A CURE FOR THE HANGOVER

Lina woke up with a mouth that felt as though something had died in it. She rolled over and tried opening one eye. She instantly regretted it. The dim light of the nebula coming through the windows seemed like a strobe light. She did a quick under-the-covers inventory. Her clothes all seemed in place, and she didn't seem damaged in any way. She ran through her memories of the evening. She wasn't quite sure how everything had gone off the rails. She tried opening her eyes again, blinking as they watered painfully, and then settled back down again. Across the cabin she could see Sparrow in the opposite bunk, his back to her.

The bunks had little pop-out side tables, and on hers was a factory-sealed water pouch, her communications bracelet, a plate with two squares of chocolate, and a med-scanner. She picked up the med-scanner and read the most recent diagnosis. *Biochemical interaction resulting in psychotropic side effects.* She pulled up the relevant chemical compounds. The first was a chemical identified as having relevant impacts on psychic activity; the second she didn't recognize. She poked at the med scanner until she identified the compound by its common name: *extract of diarvin pepper.*

She felt a swell of relief. Sparrow couldn't have known. He hadn't done it on purpose. It didn't change the fact that she'd massively violated the rules and his poor brain by shoving a memory into it, but at least neither of them had been purposely attempting to hurt the other. She sat up, slapped on her com bracelet, opened the water, and ate a piece of the chocolate. As usual, chocolate made things better. She still felt as though she'd been run over by a Qw'Adeen rock crusher and her brain kind of hurt, but chocolate existed, so maybe the world wasn't going to end.

Across the room, Sparrow turned over and sat up. He looked guilty, worried, and like he hadn't slept much. They stared at each other. Lina couldn't risk a *reading*, but she thought he also looked like he was waiting for her to speak.

She downed the rest of the water pouch and set it down. "So," she said, clearing her throat. "No more diecohol for me."

"I didn't know it would do that," he said.

"Neither did I."

He jumped down from his bunk and crossed the room, relief registering in his face.

"I'm really sorry. I guess that kills the idea of trying to sell it." He was trying for light-hearted and almost making it. His hair was sticking up where he'd been lying on it. She resisted the urge to put out a hand and smooth it down.

"No, you'll just have to put a warning label on it for people like me."

He hesitated. "People like you? It wouldn't do that to everyone from Earth?"

Lina reached nervously for the second piece of chocolate. Some of the colonies didn't deal well with her kind. She didn't want him to hate her. "No. Just those who rate on the telepathic and empathic scale. Like, um, me. Earth experimented with its own kind of modifications a few centuries ago. We're no longer, um, made, but the genes are still in the population, and occasionally we show up."

He was staring at her. She could feel the chocolate starting to melt on her fingertips, and she shoved it in her mouth.

"That's how you did the"—he touched his head—"thing."

"I'm really sorry," she said around the mouthful of chocolate, blushing.

"Why? It was amazing."

"I put a thought in your head," she said, trying to explain. "A memory. If the Registry finds out . . . I'll be punished."

He looked horrified. "Why? No. I won't let them."

She blushed again. His protectiveness came through even without an active *reading*. "I'm glad you liked it. But what if I had given you something . . . not nice? It's one thing to run an illusion on someone, like I did to those guards back at the To'Andan base. That's like hypnotism. As soon as I stop doing it, they stop thinking it. But what I did, that will stay with you."

"Good," he said.

She took a deep breath. She could feel him being stubborn at her. Should she be able to feel him this much? Had giving him a memory linked them in some way? Or was this a lingering effect of the diecohol? She rubbed her head. It was throbbing.

"I'm sorry," he said, reaching up and touching her face, his fingers gentle against her temple. "I'll stop being difficult. Yes, I see what you mean. I understand the rule. But I saw sky and birds and ocean. I was at the beach, and I will not let anyone punish you for giving me that."

"Just don't tell anyone," she said, closing her eyes and struggling not to lean into his hand. "We'll probably be fine."

"Lina," he said, and she realized it was the first time he'd ever said her name.

The ship jolted as though it had been slammed into a wall, cutting off whatever he'd been about to say next. An alarm went off, and a red light began to pulse from the cockpit. The gravity shut off, and Lina floated from the bed. Sparrow grabbed the edge of the bed and activated his boots. He ran to the cockpit and she pushed off the ceiling, angling after him. The front window was a mass of asteroids clustered against a vibrating energy field.

"What the hell is that?" demanded Lina.

"Moliter rock fence," he said, pushing buttons at a furious rate. "They're attempting to scoop valuable asteroids out of To'Andan space. Unfortunately, if we can't pull out of it, we're going to get smashed by every asteroid coming up behind us. Or ground to dust when our forward shield gives out."

"What can I do?" she asked.

"I'm going to open the engine room, flood it with gas from the nebula, mix in some oxygen, and try to ignite it. The engine room is fireproof. The explosion should push us up and over the energy field. I'm going to need you to help ignite the gas."

Lina took a second to absorb that. It sounded incredibly dangerous, but it wasn't as though she had a better idea. "Tell me what to do."

"Go to the engine room. Shut the interior door. There's a red box next to it. I'm going to need you to open it and swap two of the command chips, and then I'll open the emergency hatch and let the gas in."

"On it," she said and shoved off, sailing through the living quarters. She pulled herself through the door to the engine room, which was separated from the living quarters by a small antechamber with a viewing window into engineering. She opened the nearby red box and flipped on the coms. "What chips am I switching?" she asked.

"There should be a blue and a yellow chip. Swap them."

"Done," she said, shoving the yellow chip into place. She moved back into the antechamber and shut and sealed the door between it and the engine room.

"Opening the exterior door now," he said. She clung to the handle by the door and watched the maintenance hatch opening. Gas and small asteroids from the nebula flooded in. The gas began to condense around the equipment and drip downward. The space rocks and debris floated aimlessly, bumping into things. "Angling the ship now."

The thrusters fired, and there was a grinding noise as the ship rotated against the mash of asteroids in front of them. There was a second whoosh as he fired the thrusters to slow and stop their rotation. Then she heard the heavy click, clunk of his boots as he ran through the living quarters to join her.

"What's wrong with the gravity? Or is this the wrong time to ask?"

"Same thing that's wrong with the thrusters. The ship had to divert power to the forward shield to keep us from being crushed. Should come back on once we're clear. All right." He pulled a tool belt from a secured location on the wall and strapped it on, then grabbed her by the waist and pushed her up to the ceiling. "Above the door, there's a small panel." He pulled a panel-popper off his belt and handed it up to her. Then he knelt down by the door and popped a similar panel off. "On my mark, I want you take the yellow tube and pinch it off and hold it until . . . well, hopefully until something explodes."

"Got it." She popped the panel and waited.

"And on three, two, one, mark."

Lina pinched, and one second later there was a spark in the light fixture inside the engineering room. The resulting fireball blew out the emergency hatch and shoved the ship upward. But there was a second noise—a loud thump and twang as a base-ball-sized asteroid, fired by the explosion, slammed into the wall near the emergency hatch, punched through the interior wall, and peeled away a panel of the ship's exterior sheeting.

Lina looked at Sparrow. She really hoped he had a plan, be-cause this was outside her area of expertise. He looked like he was mentally running through a list of swear words.

Without saying any of them, he sprinted forward to the cock-pit, and moments later the emergency hatch began to close. It was sealing as he ran back again. Not that the closed door was doing much good. The atmosphere was still streaking out through the hole in the panel. She could hear the life support system going into overdrive trying to compensate. Lina tried to calculate how much longer they had until it overheated and died.

"What has to happen to fix that?" she demanded, pointing through the window into engineering.

"Uh . . . Dura-Shield Putty attached with cold-heat gun to cover the sheeting, then a hole sealer for the actual hole," he said.

"Do we have those things?"

He stared into the room as if trying to decide the answer. "Yes," he said, at last. "The hole sealer is in that cabinet." He pointed through the window at a cabinet by the water tank in the engineering room. "Dura-Shield is under the bench. I've got the cold-heat gun." He touched a tool on his belt. She could see a similar tool attached to the engineering bench inside.

"So we go in, we put on the Dura-Shield stuff, and then use the hole sealer."

"No," he said, shaking his head. "*We* don't do anything. That hole is sucking atmosphere and everything else that isn't nailed down. I've got the boots. I go in. You stay here."

Lina wasn't sure about this plan, but he was already through the door. He pulled a breather off the wall and strapped it on. He grabbed sheets of a plastic-looking material from a compartment under the engineering bench and made his way to the hole. Lina looked from the sheets to the hole and began to worry.

There was a second breather on the wall. If she could find some way to keep herself from being sucked out the hole, she could help. She went back to the living quarters and looked around. There didn't seem to be any tethers—just her damn wedding dress.

Inspiration struck and she pushed off the wall, soaring into the galley. Seizing a knife from the magnetized rack, she pushed back toward engineering. Snatching the green underdress as she went by, she angled and slid through the door to the engineering antechamber like thread through a needle. She set to cutting strips of the dress. Soon she had a long rope. She tied it to the handle bolted near the door, then tied the other end around her waist and opened the interior door.

She was sucked through instantly and hit with a face-full of condensed nebula gas. She made a grab for the breather but missed it, stopping herself on the engineering bench. Going back wasn't an option, so she'd have to make do. The life-support system was still pumping some oxygen into the room, but it was like breathing in a hurricane. She grabbed the cold-heat gun and let herself go, sailing toward Sparrow and the hole. She hit the wall and he looked down at her in surprise. She grabbed a sheet of the Dura-Shield from his hand and watched him for a second.

The method seemed to be to run the gun over the sheet and stretch it out. Wrapping one foot around his to anchor herself, she knelt down and copied his movements, working from the bottom of the hole up as he worked from the top down. She reached for a second sheet. The condensed gas was making everything slippery. Each sheet of the putty lessened the hurricane in the room but intensified the sucking toward the central hole. She reached for another sheet of putty and realized they were down to the last two. She took a calculated look at the exposed area. Two sheets wasn't going to cover it. She held up her com bracelet and ran a scan. Did they have a substitute in the room?

Her com bracelet responded, and Lina stared at the results. She looked up at Sparrow. He looked back through the breather. "I need your shirt!" she yelled, but the words were sucked away.

She reached out and tried to put the words into his head. He stared at her some more. Then he ripped his breather off and yanked his shirt off over his head. Already soaked in the gases floating around the room, her com bracelet said that it didn't need any additional ingredients. She slapped the shirt on the perforated interior wall and began to work over it with the cold-heat gun. Unlike the Dura-Shield Putty, it didn't stretch—it shrank—but it did appear to be working. He worked the other end of the shirt, but they both could tell it wasn't going to be enough. She ripped off her shirt, and he began to tack it down. The pull was already significantly lessened.

He yelled something she couldn't hear, then pointed toward the water tank. The hole sealer. He'd said it was in a cupboard. He grabbed her by the waist, pointed her in the right direction, and threw her. She sailed across the room and grabbed the cupboard, yanking open the door. The contents began to float free. She snatched the hole sealer and prepared for the return trip.

She pushed the thought that she was coming at his brain, and he reached up just in time to grab her. He pulled her down in front of him, locking one leg to the wall in front of her and over hers, holding her in place, keeping her from flying free. Together they slammed the hole sealer onto the wall, cranking the handle, expanding the seal until it covered the hole. The sucking force abruptly stopped, and then the gravity kicked back on, dropping them on the decking.

They were both gasping for air, slick with condensation, and shaking. They stared at the hole, seemingly unable to move. It felt as if every piece of her body was glued to a part of him.

Gingerly, he unlocked his foot from the wall and released his death grip on her waist. She took a deep breath and slid off his lap and onto the floor. She wasn't sure what she was supposed to say post-topless-emergency-situation.

She felt his hand brush her hair away from her back. She knew immediately what he was looking at: her clan tattoos.

"You have wings," he said. His voice sounded strange.

"You're not supposed to see those." Her voice sounded hoarse.

The air contained the distinctive burned-metal smell of space and the strangely fragrant smell of methylene. On her wrist, her com bracelet began to flash a warning light. "That's a radiation diagnostic," she said. Apparently, Nebula gases weren't good to bathe in. "We need to decontaminate."

"Damn," he said. He hauled her up to her feet and out of the engineering room. She didn't make it very far before her tether yanked her back. She tried to untie the knot, but her fingers fumbled and she let out a frustrated growl. He grabbed a knife off his belt and sliced her free, then pulled her into the bathroom. Pushing her into the shower, he stepped in beside her and began to press buttons on the shower panel. Her com bracelet was flashing rapidly as a thick, viscous liquid began to rapidly fill the shower stall.

"Radiation detox," he said, as it climbed to waist level. "I don't think there's enough for two complete doses. We're going to have to share."

She nodded as the liquid climbed past her breasts. "How long does it take?" she asked, as it climbed up to her collarbone.

"One minute," he said. He bent at the knees so that his face was at the same level as hers. They each took a deep breath as the liquid rose to their chins, and Lina closed her eyes, letting the liquid close over her head. The liquid felt like pudding. It pressed against her everywhere. She tried to stay calm, tried to hold her air in as long as possible, but she could feel a bubble of panic threatening to burst. She felt blinded and trapped. Instinctively she reached for Sparrow. He wrapped his arms around her, holding her tight to him, and somehow that was infinitely better than floating alone.

Just when she thought her lungs would explode, the pudding began to recede and the shower came on, rinsing them in lukewarm water. She didn't move. Neither did he.

She could feel him in her head. She didn't remember when she'd opened a connection between them, but it was there all the same. She felt she'd been less intimate with previous lovers than she was with him at this moment.

"Well," he said, clearing his throat. In her head she could feel him trying to figure out how to separate but not actually wanting to. "That's one way to start the day."

She looked up at him, the shower water catching in her eyelashes. "I can think of another one," she said, and brushed her lips over his.

Chapter 9:

Sparrow had stopped thinking sometime about an hour ago—about the same time their pants came off. They were now in a tangled mass on the couch. Lina had her face against his neck, and he was enjoying the feeling of her breath against his skin.

"Are you asleep?" she asked.

"Possibly," he said without opening his eyes.

She said "OK," which was a weird word she seemed to use as both an affirmative and a placeholder for everything, and snuggled more tightly against him. He loved the feeling of her skin touching his. It had been a long time since he'd had this much-prolonged contact with anyone. It finally occurred to him to wonder why she had asked.

"Did you want something, or was that a group activity check?"

"I wanted to know if we should be doing something, ship-wise."

"Probably. But I think we could probably take a moment to recover, don't you?"

"From what? The multiple life-threatening emergencies or the, uh . . . interplanetary relations?"

"Is that what we're calling it?" he asked.

"I'm definitely exploring"—she ran her hand down his side—"the Ránfuglar, and learning more"—she began to nibble his earlobe—"about some of their cultural drives"—her hand moved further downward—"and imperatives."

"Back in school we called it *testing the S-drive*, but you can fancy it up however you want," he said. He could feel her rib cage flex against him as she laughed. He sat up slightly, propping himself up on one elbow, and looked down at her naked body.

"I did just think of one thing that's going to be a problem," he said as he brushed a hand along her hip. Maybe she had it right with drives and imperatives—she definitely felt like one of those. All of those?

"Don't be ridiculous," she said, closing her eyes and adjusting slightly to make herself more available to him. "We just fixed a spaceship with our T-shirts. We can fix anything."

"Yes, except I only have one more shirt," he said.

Her eyes flew open, staring at him, and then she burst out laughing.

"Glad you think it's funny. I'm just saying it's going to be a bit awkward when we rendezvous with your ship."

"It's fine," she said, still chuckling. "I'll just chop the top off the wedding dress. The only awkward part will be when I have to explain why you have to come along and undress me."

"You don't have anyone aboard ship to work the buttons?" he asked, kissing along her collarbone.

"No," she said. "I usually work my own buttons aboard ship."

"No one volunteered for the job?" He continued to kiss her neck as his hands strayed over the curves of her body.

"Sure, but you don't get the assignment just by volunteering. How do I know if someone's got the skills for the job? And what about professional jealousy? I can't have that kind of friction among the crew."

"Understandable." He didn't say anything else as his mouth was occupied fully with hers for the next few minutes.

"What about you?" she asked when he had moved on to the other side of her neck. "Do you have any other button-handling commitments?"

"I just spent six months on To'Andan Prime," he said sitting up a bit and answering her real question. "Trust me, I have zero commitments. It's a little hard to meet anyone when you don't come home for six to nine months at a time and don't stick around when you do." He didn't add that since his accident he'd been reluctant to let other people touch him. The occasional searing pain of overactive nerves tended to make romantic moments less romantic.

Lina looked as though she was going to respond, but they both heard a rather urgent *beep* from the cockpit. "I believe the ship thinks we've had our moment of recovery," she said.

He laughed and got up. He would have to come back to this conversation. He probably shouldn't have said any of that. Just because his life was weird previously didn't mean he didn't want to pursue something with her. The thought stopped him. Did he want to do that? When was the last time he'd wanted something, let alone a relationship? But even if he did want her, what was she supposed to do—stay here? It didn't sound like that was in her job description. He stared blankly at the flashing light on the console.

He flipped the alarm off and looked at the readings. The ship was letting him know that the interior atmosphere had been fully restored. Systems weren't running at optimal, but they were within parameters. They were still on course and running on time to make the ninety-hour mark for the rendezvous.

He looked back into the living area. She hadn't moved from the couch.

If nothing else, he had the next seventy-eight hours. He should make the most of them and stop thinking about the future, because obviously there wasn't one. At least he was used to that idea.

Chapter 10:

THE AMBASSADOR WORRIES ABOUT HER BRAIN

Twelve hours into her affair with a Ránfuglar spy, Lina was quite satisfied with her decision. In fact, she'd been satisfied multiple times in several locations. They'd given up pretending they were going to put clothes back on. She had started to craft a top out of the wedding dress but had been interrupted partway through. It was now in a crumpled heap on the floor next to the table, where she had abandoned it when it was decided that they needed the table space.

In fact, practically the only location that hadn't been exposed to the indignity of their naked backsides was the actual sleeping bunks, which were narrow, too close to the ceiling, and generally uncomfortable for anything active. It was also where they were currently spooned together and trying to actually sleep. Lina was drifting in the between space of dream and awake, and she could tell by his breathing that Sparrow was close to the same. She relaxed more deeply as he rubbed his hand along the tattoo on her shoulder.

Why can't I see it?

Lina's eyes popped open.

"What?" she asked.

"Hm?"

"Did you say something?" She twisted around to look at him.

"No." He blinked at her in sleepy confusion.

Lina lay back down and tried to relax. Perhaps if that had

been the only time today she'd heard his thoughts, she might have been able to go back to sleep, but it wasn't. She waited until he was asleep and climbed down from the bed. She set her com bracelet to run an internal scan, then found the med-scanner and sat down on the couch while it did the same. Neither of the two devices was the last word in medical technology, but they ought to be able to come up with something.

The scans were still running when she became aware that Sparrow was awake and worried.

"I'm fine," she said.

"Yes, because running scans on yourself is totally normal," he said, watching her from the bunk.

Her bracelet displayed first. The readings were within her normal parameters. The med-scanner beeped and showed that she was considered healthy. She put the scanner down in disgust.

"What's going on?" he asked.

"What do you know about telepaths?"

"Not a lot. The Moliter have some skill in that direction, but I've never experienced it firsthand. We have some basic defense training on the topic before going into the field, but that's about it."

"On Earth, empaths and telepaths are rated on the Stillwell Scale from one to ten. Empaths are generally a one to four. Telepaths are fives on up. I'm a six. We're all on a list and monitored by the Bureau of Psychic Registry. Anyone above a seven and a half has more severe monitoring or lives at the Registry itself. Which sounds restrictive, but honestly most telepaths above a seven and a half have mental health problems, and living in a quiet spot where people know how to not broadcast is preferable. The general population worries that telepaths are going to be reading their thoughts. What people don't get is that most telepaths are worried about the same thing, because we don't really want to. Humans are messy thinkers. We think everything, all the time, all at once, with so much emotion and prejudice, and being exposed to that constantly is like standing in a crowded room and having people shout things at you. And if things get carried away—you know how you have my memory now?"

He nodded.

"Well, if I were to fiddle around in someone's brain too much, it's entirely possible for me to end up taking some of them back with me. Only the things that stick around are usually the bad things—the pain, the anger, the hatred."

He made an understanding but displeased noise.

"So usually I'll take a quick *reading* of the room. I check what everyone's thinking and feeling. If someone is feeling excessively contrary to what they're presenting, then I'll investigate a little bit. Sometimes it turns out that someone is just an introvert who gets flop sweats at public speaking but is good at hiding it. Sometimes someone really is lying to me. Mostly it's just politics."

"Must make you good at your job," he said.

"I guess," she said with a shrug. "But my mentor didn't have a bit of the Gift, and he could get almost what I could just from body language. So it helps; it is a short-cut, but it's not infallible. I can still be misled. I can't just look at someone and tell why they're lying to me. Maybe it's because of something I don't care about. Maybe it's because there's a bomb under the table."

"Can't you *read*—or whatever you call it—deeper and find out?"

"Yes, but I need time and the ability to concentrate. Multitasking is more of a seven ability. Also, it's considered very rude. Not alerting other parties that there's that level of telepathic activity in the room is . . . not illegal everywhere, but certainly taboo. So what I do is sort of open the door and wait for the thoughts to come popping out of people. My problem is that since our little experiment with the diecohol I'm having a hard time shutting the door. And sometimes even when it is shut I still hear what you're thinking."

"Like the salt," he said, climbing down.

"What?" She frowned at him.

"At lunch. I wanted the salt, and you gave it to me. Only I never asked for it."

She let out a little snort of exasperation. "Yes, exactly like that."

He dropped onto the couch next to her, appearing to think about what she'd said. "Am I really annoying?" he asked, and she laughed.

"No, surprisingly not. I've had similar problems after"— she hesitated, picking her words carefully to go around the classified bits—"incidences of overuse." He looked amused. "And usually everyone is just really damn irritating and everything bombards me, but this isn't like that. Or you aren't like that. I don't know."

"Well, what do you think the problem is?"

"Either the diecohol has lingering side effects, which the med-scanner does not indicate . . ."

"Those aren't exactly the finest tools in the universe," he said. "And they're not calibrated for Earth issues. It could be missing something."

"True. But my com bracelet, while also not a real medical tool, is at least calibrated for my physiology, and it's coming up negative too. The other option"—she hesitated again, this time because it was bad news—"is that I did something when I was in your head."

"So it's possible that we're more permanently connected than you'd like?"

"Or I somehow broke myself and now I'm going to have a hard time shutting everyone out, and I just don't know it because you're the only one here."

"Hm," he said. He got up and went to the galley for a water pouch. "Will your ship have more expertise on either of those fronts?"

"They have more medical equipment, certainly. If Dr. Katz doesn't come up with anything, then I'll probably have to call someone from the Registry for a consultation. Which I'm not particularly willing to do, since what I did was a violation."

"Please stop saying that," he said, irritation coloring his tone. "It makes it sound like you hurt me, and you didn't."

"Against the rules," she offered, following him into the galley.

"Sure. I'll take that. We're rebels." She smiled, because he didn't look much like a rebel. He looked like a yummy naked man with his hair sticking up. "Would it help if I tried to stop thinking at you? I can shut down more."

Lina inhaled sharply as Sparrow unexpectedly withdrew mentally. She rubbed her arm uncomfortably and looked around the room for her clothes. She hadn't realized she was quite so used to him buzzing away at the edge of her consciousness like white noise, but now that it was gone, the room felt colder. It felt more like the last time she was at home with her mother.

"Yeah, maybe," she said, trying look someplace that wasn't him.

"No," he said, setting down his water and stepping closer, pulling her to him. "No, I'll stop." She inhaled the smell of his skin as he came back to her. "There, see?" He kissed her as she put her arms around him, holding him tight, wanting to feel his warmth again. "Back to normal."

Was it normal? Shouldn't he be wanting to shut her out more? Her mother had been a fleet admiral with secrets to protect and the training to do so, and she used that training consistently whenever Lina was home. Why she thought shutting Lina out so hard was necessary, Lina had never been quite able to emotionally understand, but emotions never really counted for much with her mother. But Sparrow was a spy. Presumably he had as much reason as, if not more than, her mother to shut her out. But instead, he felt open. If this was his normal, then she wished it could be her normal too.

Chapter 11:

THE SPY CONTEMPLATES THE PAST

They ended up back on the couch because that was the biggest piece of furniture, and while it was shorter than the bunks, the width was better for both of them. This time, when she dropped off to sleep, she didn't wake back up. Sparrow, on the other hand, found himself wide awake.

He'd never considered the problem of telepathy with any seriousness before. He'd seen what the Moliter had done to spies they caught. But there weren't telepaths among the population the way Lina made it sound when she told him about the Terrans. And it had never occurred to him that telepaths might have problems simply interacting with everyone or maintaining their own headspace. He supposed the second he'd realized what she was, he should have run through all of his training and shut down as much as possible. That would certainly be the recommended course of action. Or rather, that would certainly be what Tanager would have him do. And maybe if he'd simply been told she was telepathic, he might have. Instead she'd given him waves and sand, and he found that he couldn't fear her with that in his head. And her face when he'd blocked her . . .

Sparrow decided to let his decision stand. They had until they met her crew, and he was going to try and enjoy every minute, because as soon as they set foot aboard her ship, they would both have to go back to work.

He pulled a blanket over both them and went to sleep.

When he opened his eyes again, she was sitting up, her arms around her knees, staring out the window above them, her back on full display. She had two wings, one on each shoulder blade. Beneath each wing, smaller designs trailed down on either side of her spine.

"They're clan tattoos," she said, without turning around. "It's traditional in my family that only those in the clan should see the tattoos on the back. Although I don't usually show them when I'm home, either. My mom is still pissed about the wings."

"Why?" he asked.

"It's traditional to take an older, prominent family member—which would certainly be my mother—with you to get the first ones done. I didn't. I knew that if I took her, I would end up getting what she thought was the right thing and not what I wanted."

"Why did you want wings?"

She was silent for a long moment, still watching the nebula. "There is more to the memory I gave you. That was the day I found out that I had the Gift. I saw an eagle hunting. Eagles are large birds of prey. They eat fish and small animals. And I saw it swoop down close to me, and I was fixated on it. I'd never seen one that close before. And when it took off again, I went with it. I spent the rest of the day being an eagle. When I finally got back to my body, I had to remember how to walk again. And it took me forever to get home and I was sick for a week afterward and I had to go Registry sleep-away camp. Turns out that going out in someone else's brain is about the least safe way to discover you're Gifted. I could have easily not made it back. But the thing is, I have never regretted that day. Flying with the wind in my face and the world beneath me . . ."

Sparrow felt the intense rush of longing that he thought he had gotten over. He tried to push it back down so she wouldn't feel it too. Wouldn't feel the way the world would fall away as he lifted. The way everything was both silent and loud with the wind in his ears. Wouldn't feel the snap of his wings opening or the sensation of being supported by an invisible hand.

"I've always wanted to be, to have, that again. The tearing off chunks of mouse, not so much. But the flying, I want that. I tried once to tell my mom it was an important day to me, and she just said that almost dying the first time always feels important."

"What in the seven hells of the Moliter does that mean?"

"She's a bona fide war hero, so I think she meant that she's almost died lots and it's not that big of a deal. But that isn't what made the day important for me. I didn't even know I could have died until they told me later. Ultimately, I think it just meant that to her my experiences aren't very important."

"That is drang *skit.*"

"I'm not sure what drangs are how much *skit* they produce, but yes. Which is why I didn't take her to get my tattoos. But since you were there too in a sense, I think you should be able to look at them."

She looked over her shoulder at him, and he felt his stomach do little flip-flop. It was enough to tell him that his plan to leave everything here in the *Ember* might not be as easy as he'd been thinking it would be.

"I can't tell what you're thinking," she said, looking amused to be saying it.

"I was thinking that your mother and my father would have been the best of friends. *Get up. Get over it. Stop lying around.* Dad, my spine is crushed, I literally can't. *You're moping. Life isn't over. Soldiers keep marching.* Because they can *fjandinn* walk, Dad.

"Amazingly, that didn't actually carry any weight with him."

"Can I punch him for you?" she offered, crawling back up the length of the couch to lie next to him.

"I'd settle for punching him myself," he said. "Or, you know, just arguing like we used to. He died about seven years ago."

"I'm sorry!" She hugged him, and maybe it was his imagination, but he felt her hugging sympathy into his brain.

"Our relationship was never very good. He and Tanager always saw eye to eye, but with me, we never seemed to look at anything from the same point of view. But you always think that maybe someday you'll finally connect. Then one day he was gone, and so was the possibility that we'd ever get it right."

"I suddenly want to call my mother," she said.

He laughed. "Maybe you'll have better luck than I did."

"How did you break your back?"

"A flying accident," he said, because that was true, if nonspecific. "I couldn't walk for about a year."

"That must have been really frightening."

"It took away a lot," he said. "I don't think my family ever got how much. And then, miraculously, I got better and they thought I should just be the same as before. Like getting over a cold. It doesn't really work like that."

"How'd you get better?" she asked, and he kicked himself. This was exactly the sort of thing Tanager would tell him to stop talking about.

"Cybernetic implants," he said. Again, true, if nonspecific.

"Really?" She adjusted to look up at him, surprised. He nodded. "Hm. That's an underdeveloped field for us. The Naturalists managed to enact a lot of laws in the early days that put cybernetic research on hold."

"Is it still illegal on Earth?" he asked. Tanager would want to know.

"Honestly, I have no idea. With bioengineering having advanced as it has, I just think the focus is there. I can look it up when we get back to the *Tempest*." She was staring at the ceiling thoughtfully. She'd had the same expression when listening to Queen Maarta.

"I was trying to be personal, not tell you about future negotiating points," he said.

"Right," she said, blinking. "Right. I am not thinking about work."

"I shouldn't have asked whether it was illegal," he said.

"But you thought it would be useful to know?" Her eyes crinkled up in laughter.

"Yes," he admitted.

"We should probably have some sort of work meeting today and cover things we're supposed to be talking about." She said it with a sigh, like she didn't really want to.

"There's time for that later," he said, unwilling to relinquish a minute of his time with her to work.

"Later," she agreed, with a smile.

Chapter 12:

THE AMBASSADOR MEETS A PIRATE

Oh, how frightened little Thumbelina felt when the cockchafer flew with her to the tree! But especially was she sorry for the beautiful white butterfly which she had fastened to the leaf, for if he could not free himself he would die . . .

Hans Christian Andersen, Thumbelina

"I forgot how much this pushed my boobs up," said Lina, surveying herself the mirror.

"I didn't," said Sparrow, passing by the bathroom on the way to the engine room. He had put on clothes, for some reason.

She had hacked the skirt off the dress, ripped out the sleeves, folded down the ridiculous collar, and removed a few of the chains and sparkles, but nothing could change the basic bosom-empha-sizing construction. The resulting top was a bit piratical.

"I look like I should be flogging the cabin boy."

"Sounds good," said Sparrow, going back the other way car-rying the tool belt. Lina chuckled.

"I don't think flogging means what you want it to mean," she yelled over her shoulder into the cabin.

"*Can* it mean what I want it to mean?" he yelled back.

"Yes," she said, laughing. She wondered if living with him

would be like this—mostly naked and laughing all the time. She brushed and then began to braid her hair as she contemplated her love life—which was nonexistent, mostly, interspersed with the occasional temporary entertainment.

The sound of a running saw came from the other room. He was up to something, but she chose not to investigate mentally, preferring to be surprised.

She had intended that their interlude be limited to their time here on this tiny ship. His comments and passing thoughts indicated that he felt the same. And usually by this point in a week's entertainment, she was slightly bored and ready to move on. So everything should have been fine. But they were inching past the halfway mark, and she was already dreading the coming deadline. She wanted more time. She finished her braid and looked in the mirror. It wasn't as if she had much more to offer him. She didn't exactly have a stick-around kind of job. And what would he do if he came with her?

She had just determined that things were what they were—there was nothing she could do about it and she should just go out there, enjoy some flogging, and relish every minute they had left—when the entire ship shuddered. She staggered to the bathroom door in time to see him sprinting to the cockpit. She ran after him but the ship shuddered again, throwing her onto the couch. She had time to register that he'd sawed the couch in half, laying down the back and making a larger, wider bed for them, when the ship shook again. This time, she heard a distinct crack.

She ran to the cockpit and found him applying thrusters and swearing. The coms crackled with an incoming message, playing on a loop.

"Your ship is now property of the Be'attle Corps. Surrender and we may let you live."

"Sure, and be sold into slavery. No, thanks," muttered Sparrow. He punched a few more buttons, and the ship creaked ominously.

"What is the Be'attle Corps?" asked Lina.

"Pirates. They call themselves *corps* as if they're legitimate salvagers, but they're raiders, plain and simple. And they've got us in a gravity loop. If we can't break free, they'll tear us apart."

"What do we do?"

"I can trigger a feedback frequency in the loop, but I need more time. If we don't respond soon, they're going to start shooting."

Lina pulled up the display and located the pirate ship. It was about a kilometer away, barely within view amid the drifts of the nebula. It was a long reach for her, but maybe if she had face-to-face contact . . .

"How do I contact them? Can I get a visual on them?"

Sparrow reached over and flipped two switches. "Red button, then blue."

Lina pressed as commanded and a screen popped up. It wasn't even three-dimensional. She hoped it would be enough.

"I'm Captain Chafre," said a man coming onto the screen. He was working with some body modification art in the way of metal antennae. They waved at her independently as he spoke. Lina tried to ignore them and concentrate. "Your vessel is now under our control. You will surrender." Surprisingly, it was easier than she had expected. His mind was right there in front of her. He tasted metal and felt lemon. When their senses started to overlap, it meant she was stretching her Gift a bit too far, but she ignored the sensation.

"Captain, it's so lovely to meet you," she said, flipping rapidly through his brain, trying to find where he kept the love and attraction. Filed under Money, of course. Sparrow glanced up but didn't say anything. "My name is Lina Tum-Bel."

"Lina?" he repeated, stammering slightly.

"I'm sooo excited to find someone who understands the potential of making profit."

"Profit," he repeated, sighing the word in true love.

"I have a proposition for you, Captain Chafre, but you need to release the gravity loop so we can talk."

"I'm not sure," he said, shaking his head. The antenna swayed angrily, as if sensing that the brain under them was misbehaving.

"Aren't I beautiful? Don't I have lots of shiny money? Don't you want that?"

"Yes," he sighed.

She pushed harder. "Then you need to release the gravity loop."

"I need to release the gravity loop," he said.

"Yes," she agreed. "You're wise to do so."

He nodded. "Release the gravity loop!" he bellowed to someone off screen. There was a chatter of disagreement. "Idiot!" he yelled, and for a moment the screen went black. She could feel herself starting to sweat with the effort of maintaining a link without the visual.

The gravity loop abruptly shut off, and the *Ember* leaped forward. Sparrow applied thrusters, and the ship lurched into the mist.

"How long do we have?" he demanded, flipping switches. The lights in the cabin went off as he cut and rerouted power. It wasn't going to do much good. From Captain Chafre's mind, she knew the Be'attle ship was much faster.

"Not long," she said. She closed her eyes and tried to block out distractions and keep the link with the captain in her head. He was arguing with his crew. Abruptly, the link went dead. The shock knocked her out of her chair and she bit her tongue.

Sparrow picked her up and set her back in the copilot chair. The firm pressure of his hands was steadying. "I think the crew knocked him out," she said. "They'll be coming after us." He nodded his acknowledgement but didn't respond otherwise.

He pushed the ship into a thick cloud of gas and ran back into the cabin. He had shifted into working mode. He felt to her the way he had at the To'Andan base—focused and moving fast. He had some sort of plan, but she didn't know what it was. She looked around the cockpit. She didn't know what to do or how to help.

He came running back to the cockpit. "Send another transmission to your ship," he said. "Give them the following coordinates." He punched up some numbers, and Lina copied them into her com and hit Send.

"Why?" she asked. He lifted her bodily from the chair and pushed her into the cabin. "They won't get the message in time to be any help."

"No," he agreed. There was a panel missing from the wall near the cabin door. It showed the blue-lit interior of an escape pod. "But they'll know where to find you."

He shoved her inside and slammed the door closed, which meant he didn't hear her scream.

PART III:

Of Moles, Devices, & Daughters

In the middle of the floor lay a dead swallow, his beautiful wings pulled close to his sides, his feet and his head drawn up under his feathers; the poor bird had evidently died of the cold. It made little Thumbelina very sad to see it, she did so love the little bird; all the summer he had sung and twittered for her so beautifully. But the mole pushed it aside with his crooked legs, and said, "He will sing no more now. How miserable it must be to be born a little bird! I am thankful that none of my children will ever be birds . . ."

Hans Christian Andersen, Thumbelina

Chapter 13:

THE AMBASSADOR LEAVES THE FRYING PAN AND ARRIVES IN THE FIRE

The escape pod tumbled violently, throwing Lina from wall to wall. Finally she managed to grab one of the straps that was supposed to be wrapped around her and hang on. Asteroids hit the hard shell of the pod with a pinging impact as she struggled to strap herself in. The chest strap had barely locked in place when a large rock struck the pod and fractured the outer layer of the window. She looked in horror at the spider web in the glass, and then she looked outward through the glass and realized she had bigger problems.

An asteroid the size of small moon appeared through the mist of the nebula, and she was heading straight for it. The pod spun, showing ever-larger flashes of the approaching asteroid. Pulling against the centrifugal force, she slammed her legs into the bed and activated the pod's crash sequence. The last thing she saw through the cracked window, as she felt the straps anchor her in place and the crash pads inflate, was the briefest glimpse of the *Ember* speeding away, pursued by the Be'attle pirate ship.

When she awoke, she was not entirely certain that she had opened her eyes. Wherever she was lying was soft, fluffy, and entirely dark. She moved her hands outward and found the edge of the softness and then empty air. She felt downward and found what felt to be the edge of a bed. She reached outward with her mind, looking for someone living. She found one mind, but pulled back almost instantly. The mind was a mess of *yes, no, maybe, what to do, what to do, what to do.* Lina shut down access and was relieved to find that her mind obeyed. Perhaps her problems with Sparrow were limited to Sparrow.

At the thought of him, she felt an overwhelming burst of panic and reached out instinctively with her mind, searching for him. Mostly so she could tell him that he was an idiot. But yelling at him very much required that he be alive, and she was not at all certain that was the case. She opened up wider, blocking the dithering ball of incompetence that seemed to be heading her direction, and tried to feel the universe. Perhaps it was her imagination, but she thought she almost felt him. But the feeling slipped away, replaced by the unpleasant sensation that someone else was looking for her. She pulled back and was startled to discover that the ball of worry was now audible.

"I just don't know. I really don't," someone was saying as they opened a door. Lina sat up and blinked at a small pale woman with white hair outlined in the sapphire blue light of the hallway.

"What don't you know?" asked Lina. The woman jumped, making a startled *meep* noise.

"I didn't know you were awake, for one thing," said the woman, her tone scolding.

"I beg your pardon," said Lina. "I didn't mean to startle you."

"You should be more careful." The woman clapped her hands. The lights in the room flickered on, but barely at the level of a candle. "You must come along now. The count is coming, and I really don't know what I shall do if he is displeased."

"And who is the count?" asked Lina, climbing out of the bed. She was barefoot but still dressed in Sparrow's spare pants and her To'Andan wedding-dress top. But even without footwear, she towered over the woman in front of her, and she found herself looking down into a wrinkled face with eyes that took up far too much room and were the palest white, as if two moons had landed in her face.

"Well, he's the count," said the woman. "You should know better than to ask about your betters!"

"There seem to be a lot of things I should do. I had no idea. And who are you? Or should I know that too?"

"I don't see how. I'm Mimi Ouse."

"And you're friends with the count?"

"Oh, dear me, no. I should think I know my place better than to presume to be friends with such a fine gentleman as the count."

"Read a lot of Dickens, do you?" asked Lina.

"Read?" repeated Mimi. "What's that, now?"

"Right," said Lina, realizing the problems reading would pose to people with presumably few light receptors. "Well, Mimi, I would very much like to meet your count, but perhaps I might have my shoes back?" She looked around the room, hoping to see them hiding in one of the shadows.

"Oh no, I don't think we can do that," said Mimi. "We lost one in transport."

"Transport?"

"Of you, from there to here. Only the Deep Gods would know where that shoe went."

"OK," said Lina. "Barefoot it is, then. Needs must when the devil drives, and all that."

"We don't let the Devils drive here," said Mimi. "Keep them

more to cooking and cleaning."

"That sounds entirely reasonable," said Lina, which is what she always said when people were spouting nonsense.

"Yes." Mimi had the look of someone who'd lost the thread of the conversation. "Um, well, this way."

Lina followed Mimi up a corridor that rose steeply in elevation as they walked. Light emanated from the ceiling and colored everything blue. Under the blue of the hallway light, Lina could see that Mimi's eyes did have some sort of iris that moved behind the white, scanning the ground in front of her. Lina quickly found herself panting as though she were exerting ten times the effort.

Mimi noticed with a shake of her head. "Oxygen wasters, the lot of you. You should have accepted the modifications as the Deep Gods intended. But no, you know better. You see fit to waste the air they give you. Immoral is what it is."

"So it is the will of the Deep Gods that your people became modified?" Lina was trying to work her way through Mimi's ramblings.

"Of course! Do they teach you nothing? You godless robotic wonders! Always flying around here and there. Heathens! Stay in the ground like a normal person!"

"Mimi, forgive my ignorance, but what exactly do you think I am?"

Mimi squinted at her and seized her arm, rolling Lina's skin between her thumb and forefinger. "Ránfuglar, of course. Admittedly, you don't smell quite right and you're wearing the To'Andan royal crest. But what else could you be? Although the smell really is so very wrong. And there weren't any metal bits, so I don't know. I just don't know. I really don't. But I'm only a woman. So we shall see what the count says. The count will know. Yes, the count will know what to do."

Lina frowned. Sparrow had said that cybernetic implants had allowed him to walk again, but she had assumed they were for an isolated medical need. Mimi's incoherent speech suggested that cybernetics and bionics were far more widespread among the Ránfuglar than Lina had previously suspected. Lina felt a flash of annoyance—she knew she shouldn't have let Sparrow distract her so much. She should know more about the Ránfuglar by now. Her annoyance was almost immediately followed by the fear that he would never distract her again.

Lina took a surreptitious glance at her com bracelet. She had been unconscious for approximately ten hours. That put the *Tempest* approximately thirty-five hours from the rendezvous point. Unless they had arrived early and had been waiting for her? They might be looking for her now. Assuming they had received the message Sparrow had made her send. Or maybe they were thirty-five hours away from even starting to look for her.

Lina took a deep breath, attempting to steady herself. She was in a spot of trouble—that much was obvious. But panicking about it would not get her out, and it certainly would not help her find Sparrow.

Mimi continued to lead the way through a maze of halls and narrow passageways, until they arrived in a wide chamber. In the center of the floor was an outcropping of glowing white crystal the height of a man and about three people thick. Long tables were set around the chunk of crystal, in a way that reminded Lina of a fire pit in the longhouses of her ancient ancestors.

"Nice," said Lina, surveying the space.

"Really?" Mimi looked around. "I always find it too open. So much space overhead. What if the roof caves in?"

Lina looked upward at the crystal-studded ceiling. It was like being inside a geode. "Then I imagine we would die," she said. "But we would be just as dead in a smaller area."

"There's more structural integrity in smaller spaces," said Mimi, her tone implying that Lina was an idiot.

"But the cavern is natural, yes? Wouldn't that mean that the Deep Gods meant there to be a cavern here?"

Mimi was silent, and a quick *reading* told Lina that this was because she couldn't find a way to argue with Lina's statement. "Just sit down," said Mimi, pointing to a table. "We'll wait for the count here."

"Tell me about the count," said Lina, seating herself on one of the benches and pulling up her feet to sit cross-legged. "Is he a pleasant person?"

Almost no one ever described a person they liked as *pleasant*. *Pleasant* was almost universally reserved for people who might not be quantifiably objectionable but were, all the same, deserving of being fired out of an airlock. How Mimi answered the question would say a great deal about the count.

"The count is all that a proper count should be. He gives his proper tithe, and he sends his taxes to the king, and he protects us from those heathens who would harm us."

"I see," said Lina. "A proper count indeed." In her experience, only two kinds of people made a virtue of paying taxes:

people who collected them and people running for office.

She felt the count coming before he actually arrived. He felt like a thundercloud. She had spent her required year of service at the Registry. She knew what powerful telepaths felt like—massive like dreadnoughts, weighted with defenses but deadly when engaged. The count did not feel like that. He buzzed in her brain, undirected, threatening, like a temperamental toddler. There appeared to be no defenses on the count, only massive eddies of psychic energy. A spiral of anger was curling out, and as the count entered the room, two workers began to bicker. She wondered if he had any control at all or if it pleased him to have others dance to his whims. She was so busy looking at him mentally that when he stopped in front of her, she was startled to discover that he had actual form.

He was tall, with the pale moon eyes of the Moliter people, and had a sharp widow's peak of dark hair on a high forehead. He was dressed in black, and his long fingers ended in sharp nails. Behind him was an entourage that included a girl who resembled him strongly enough that Lina assumed she was his daughter.

He stared at her. She stared back.

"Your hubris is amazing," said the count. "To attempt to spy on the Moliter, I expect that from your arrogant people, but to dare to put on the crest of royalty . . . You go beyond the dark."

He oozed with disgust and condescension. Lina remained seated. The count was taller than she was. Her standing up would only emphasize their height disparity. By remaining seated, she was subtly implying that she had no need to stand in his presence.

She frowned up at him. "And who are you, that my clothing

choices should be any of your concern?"

His pale cheeks flushed with two spots of red, and a buffet of anger seeped out of the cloud.

"I am Count Talpidae. I am the chief spy hunter of the King of Moliter. You would do well to fear me."

She did fear him, but not necessarily for the reasons he thought she should. The amount of emotion rolling off of him could start a war, and while it seemed to react vaguely to him, it didn't seem under his control. She kept her defenses firmly up as she tried to examine him and his party.

"While I'm sure that is of the utmost importance to the king, it's of absolutely no interest to me," said Lina. "I am neither a spy nor Ránfuglar, as your people seem to assume. I am Ambassador Lina Tum-Bel of the Interplanetary Alliance."

"You lie," said the count, snapping his fingers. "All your people lie."

There was a shuffle at the back of the room, and four people were pushed into the room in chains. Lina recognized the pirate captain, and she assumed the other man and woman were part of his crew, but most important to her was the fourth—bloodied, bruised, but still alive: Sparrow. Lina kept herself from running to him. Despite her defenses, she could feel pain leaking off him in waves. His shoulder seemed to be at its center, and as the group drew closer she saw a piece of metal protruding from it.

"Well?" asked the count, turning to the pirate captain.

"Yes," said the captain. "That's her. She was the one in the ship."

"The Ránfuglar ship. With the Ránfuglar spy," said the count, poking Sparrow in his injured shoulder. She tried not to react to the pain he was feeling. For his part, Sparrow did not respond except to grimace in discomfort.

"I believe you mean my escort to Ránfuglar Prime," said Lina.

"I mean nothing of the kind," snapped the count, lashing out mentally. She weathered the strike—it was heavy, but unskilled and blunt. "You should tell me the truth, and I may go easy on you."

She frowned. For a man with an enormous amount of psychic energy swirling about him, he had yet to attempt to actually investigate her mind.

"I have told you the truth. And you have replied with threats and attacks. I have to warn you that my people will see any violence toward me as an attack on the Alliance and will react accordingly."

"If the *Alliance*"—he sneered the word—"actually existed, perhaps I would find that concerning. But like all your people, you lie. Take them to the cells. Take her to the Device."

"No." The word sounded as though it had been squeezed out of Sparrow's lungs. She could feel his initial impulse to step into her place—to volunteer himself—followed by growing horror at the realization that if he did, his entire family and his people might be in jeopardy.

The count smiled, and the emotions around him changed to a vicious happiness. "He knows what's waiting for you. Soon you, too, will discover the consequences of lying to me."

Chapter 14:

THE AMBASSADOR LEARNS OF THE MOLITER DEVICE

The room was lined in lead. Which was charmingly quaint in an uneducated, barbaric kind of way. Lead in no way stopped psychic powers. The only thing it had ever done was block some imaging devices, and although having images of a person or location did help telepathic contact, lead did not affect telepaths one way or another. There was a rack of sorts in the center of the room. Tubing and wires were attached to it. It was not hard to see how a person was strapped to it. What was difficult was discerning the purpose.

Still allowed freedom of movement, Lina walked around the Device. She sensed that the count thought this would build her fear. He was right. The console that controlled it seemed to lack basic failsafes. She was starting to believe that Sparrow's fears were well founded.

"Rudimentary telepathic torture device?" she guessed, looking from the machine to the count.

"Rudimentary!" he squawked. "It is the first of its kind. I am a pioneer in my field, and it is not for torture. It is a behavioral corrective device."

"The fact that you mentioned that last tells me you're lying. But we can pretend if you like. What behavior were you trying to correct?"

"Mine," said the count's daughter, her voice barely above a whisper.

"And has it worked?" asked Lina, surveying the console again. It was her guess that the machine attempted to generate a psychic episode and then drained the brain of the chemical compounds associated with those episodes.

"Yes," said the girl. "I no longer have improper thoughts."

Prolonged or repeated exposure would most likely deplete the brain, perhaps permanently, which would have permanent cognitive side effects. And, of course, the torture wasn't going to help. Lina suspected that the count's daughter was two brain cells short of a lobotomy.

"I imagine you no longer have many thoughts at all," said Lina.

"Thoughts in women are unbecoming," said the count. "Strap her to the Device."

Lina didn't resist. There wasn't much point, and she was going to need her strength.

The machine used a two-pronged approach to generate a response. Diodes strapped to nerve centers caused pain, while a chemical stream pouring into one arm pushed the brain into a psychic state. All the while, the count would ask his questions.

The problem, she suspected, was that he'd never questioned anyone with a measurable Gift before. For every question he asked, it was as if he was picturing her expected response. He started with small questions: her name, her age, her family, where she was from. For each answer he didn't like—and that was all of them—the pain scraping across her nerves increased.

After what seemed like an eternity, she finally stopped telling the truth and gave him the answers he was expecting. She was from Ránfuglar Beta; she was a spy. He sucked up the answers greedily and moved on to his real questions.

"How do the Ránfuglar fly?"

Lina sensed that he did not mean *fly* as she would mean it, but she couldn't discover another meaning. "Like everyone else," she offered. The swirl of emotions around his head was giving her nothing.

"How do they fly?" he demanded again, and this time the image in his head was crystal clear: Sparrow with wings, soaring across an orange sky. "We all know it's cybernetics. We have the basic schematics. But how does the tech interface with the brain?"

"I have no idea," said Lina, honestly.

Lina couldn't tell whether her honesty had made a dent or he didn't really expect her to know, but he sat back in disgust.

"Useless. Fine. Let's talk about the planet. Who holds the defense-line access codes?"

"Don't have a clue."

He adjusted a dial and Lina screamed.

"Let's try that again," he said, when she paused for breath. "How do we access the planet?"

In his head, she could see he was envisioning himself as the controller and possessor of the planet's untold wealth. Mines rumbling constantly; the Ránfuglar his slaves, their wings shredded and on the ground. The idea of it made him drool a little, as if he was smelling cooking meat.

"Even if I knew, I wouldn't tell you," said Lina, and he turned the dial again.

Lina realized that she didn't have to feel the pain. She could stop it, if she just left her body. Where to go was the question. The next jolt hit her and she popped out, spreading herself over the surface of the room and then along the corridors and warren of the asteroid base.

The count's daughter sat at a table in the great hall, hands in her lap, doing nothing, simply sitting. She touched the girl's mind, but no sparks answered her. It seemed there was nothing to respond with. She found Mimi, overseeing the intake of ore from the mines. Her mind was firmly trying to ignore what was happening to Lina. In the kitchen, a red-looking non-human waved one of his four arms at her with an impish ping of mental interest. That was interesting. Somewhere behind her, she could feel the count shouting at her.

She offered the equivalent of a mental handshake, and the red thing reached back. He was a Devil. Devils cleaned things. Devils liked asteroids. They were warm. They thought Moliter were stupid and of one mind. He'd never met a human who was fully two minds before. Was she a new thing? Was she a new kind of Moliter? All of that rolled into one question: *What are you?*

Lina responded the best she could. Alien first contact was not her specialty. Then she asked how to escape. The Devil's mind lit up with a blinding maze and then narrowed to one route.

Will you help me? The count is hurting me. I don't want to stay.

The devil felt perplexed and pushed out a thought of clarification. She allowed him entry. Exposing what she had felt in the machine. The Devil pulled back, chittering angrily and shaking one of his fists.

Yes. We will help.

The machine stopped and there was a sharp tug, pulling her out of the kitchen and back toward her body.

She was with her body, but not really in her body. She saw a long needle extract itself from her brain and then inject something into a small vial. She watched as the count then injected it into himself. The cloud of energy around the count pulsed, and he gasped orgasmically. Apparently, her brain juice was better than most. That didn't make her feel better.

Lina was aware that they were dragging her. She was aware when they dropped her. But she couldn't seem to get back into her body properly. It was like the first day with the eagle all over again. She was far, far gone in the sky, and down in the dark somewhere was a body that may sort have belonged to her at some point.

She was trying to decide if it was worth worrying about or if she should just move on, when she heard someone insistently calling her name. It was Sparrow. He was angry and scared and wanted her to come back.

She landed back in her own head with what felt like a physical jolt. She realized that she was lying on the floor of one of the cells. Sparrow was saying her name from somewhere. The next cell? She rolled to her back. There was a scrabbling noise as Sparrow stretched his arm through the bars, reaching out for her hand.

"Lina, *sæta*, Lina." In his head, *sæta* was an old word and an instinctual choice meaning something along the lines of *sweetie*— like a pet name between lovers. She'd never been anyone's *sæta* before. She flung out her hand and he seized it. The sense of relief from him was instantaneous, but she was unprepared for how steadying it felt to her. The prickle of sensation from his fingers to hers locked her into her body.

"How come you didn't tell me you could fly?" she whispered.

"Because I can't," he said. For an instant he was reliving his accident—the tangle of feathers, the screaming screech of metal, and the smell of burning flesh. She jerked her hand away, and she could feel him mentally scrambling to think of something else. His mind settled on chocolate and she chuckled, reaching out for his hand again.

She drifted for a few more minutes. This was going to be a problem. This drifting felt like what she'd read level nines experienced—the ability to walk out of their bodies at any time, which led to forgetting that the body needed things, which led, eventually, to death. The Registry had developed multiple engagement therapies designed to keep nines in their bodies. Their success rates were only slightly above fifty percent. Lina thought she could possibly shed some insight into the problem. At the moment, the only thing holding her here was the feeling of Sparrow's hand in hers and the rock-solid weight of his mind wanting her to stay. She might have to write a paper. Although that was rather assuming that she lived through this.

She forced her body to take a deep breath. In the forefront of Sparrow's mind was a single thought.

They are going to kill you, and I don't know how to stop them.

"I do," she said. "We're going to let the Devil drive."

Chapter 15:

THE SPY FINDS NEW ALLIES

Sparrow adjusted Lina's com bracelet on his arm and watched them take her away again. They had let her sleep for almost eight hours. He didn't think they were doing it out of kindness. They wanted her to recover enough to be questioned again.

He had seen the results of this type of questioning before. The three operatives they had recovered alive had been close to mindless vegetables. The other six were dead. And each time, the breach in their security had been enormous. The operatives had all given up everything. So far Lina hadn't revealed that he was a Ránfuglar spy, but he had no idea how long she could hold out. She said she could go further, but Sparrow was not so sure. She had said that she had to; otherwise her plan wouldn't work.

Her plan depended a lot on the help of pirates, who hated him, and the red non-human species the Moliter kept—no one knew what they hated—and his ability to get to her ship. All of which would be a lot easier to do if he didn't have a hunk of metal sticking through his shoulder. He waited until the door closed behind the guards and Lina.

"You want to get out of here?" he asked, turning to the pirates.

"How you gonna make that happen?" asked the captain, rubbing his jaw where Sparrow had punched him.

"In about a minute, someone's going to walk in here with food."

"So what? There's always a guard with them."

"In the food there will be a key card for the door. The guard is going to open the cell door instead of sticking the food through the slot. If we can take out the guard and get to the door two levels up, there will be someone waiting for us with a transport buggy. They can get us to the surface."

The pirates exchanged glances. "How do you know?"

"You felt what Lina did to you. She says there will be, so there will be."

"Yeah, I felt it. It was a load of lies in my brain. How do you know she's not lying to you too? Right now, they'll probably just sell us or put us to work in the mine, but if we try to escape they'll kill us for sure."

"I'll do it," said the woman. Sparrow had learned that she was called May, but her relationship to either of the others was unclear. The captain glared at her. "What?" continued May. "She's not going to lie to him. They're obviously *ástfanginn*."

Ástfanginn implied that not only were they in love, they were meant to be. Sparrow didn't comment on that—he couldn't even think about that right now. The third pirate nodded, and the captain grunted in annoyance.

"Fine, but getting to the surface doesn't do us any good. We need a ship."

"There will be one," said Sparrow, hoping he was telling the truth.

The plan was simple enough. In order to get off the asteroid, they needed a ship. And that meant getting the com bracelet to the surface to signal the *Tempest*. But in order to get out of their cells and get to the surface, Lina would have to run an illusion. Which, in her condition, she couldn't do while moving. That meant Sparrow would have to take the bracelet, signal the ship, and come back to get her. She had said the red Devils would provide the key to the door and the transport buggy. Sparrow had no way of judging whether they could be trusted, but he knew he couldn't trust the pirates. Unfortunately, with his left hand inoperable, he needed them. In all, Sparrow hated the plan almost as much as he hated the count.

The guard arrived and they all watched as he tried repeatedly to fit the food tray through the slot near the floor. The tray fit without problems, but he pulled it back again and again, as if it were hitting an obstruction.

"Just open the door," said the guard in the room. "They're against the far wall. It will be fine."

The captain looked at Sparrow with a glimmer of a smile. They were all clustered around the door. Lina's illusion was working.

The door swung open, and the woman grabbed the guard by the collar and head-butted him while the captain seized his sidearm. He pointed the gun and pulled the trigger, but nothing happened. The second guard blinked, seeming to struggle with what was in his mind and what was in front of him.

"It's hand locked, you *hálfviti*," said Sparrow, grabbing the food tray and hitting the second guard in the face. "It will only work for his hand." The third pirate dumped out the bowls of mush. In the third bowl was a blue crystal chip. An all-door-access passkey, usually reserved for maintenance staff.

"You're the *hálfviti*," snapped the captain. "You're the one with a metal pipe in your shoulder."

"That you stabbed me with, you *rassgat*!"

"There's no reason for that kind of language," said the third pirate, speaking for the first time, his antennae waggling gently.

"Melonotha doesn't like swearing," said the woman.

"And I keep telling him he's in the wrong *fjandinn* line of work," bellowed Chafre in Melonotha's direction.

"May," said Melonotha, looking mournfully at the woman.

The woman poked Chafre sharply in the ribs. "Shut your yap. Let's just get out of here."

It was quickly becoming apparent to Sparrow who really ran Captain Chafre's crew. They stepped cautiously out into the hallway.

Left.

Lina's voice was in his head, and he turned automatically as she told him.

"Where are you going?" demanded Captain Chafre.

"We're supposed to go this way," said Sparrow.

"I hate this psychic drang s—" May's stare bored into Chafre's skull. "Poo?" he offered, looking around.

Sparrow ignored them, trying to hold the feeling of Lina in his head. She guided them through the maze of corridors, and finally they were within sight of a blue fire door between levels. Each time they approached a Moliter inhabitant, the person magically seemed called to look somewhere else. In case of accident or emergency, any level could be isolated and the air evacuated, putting out any fires. Also killing anyone who happened to be on the level, but those were the decisions that had to be made when you lived on an asteroid.

Suddenly there was a searing jolt of pain running down his right side, and the tenuous silver thread that Lina felt like in his mind disappeared. In the distance, they all heard the echo of a scream. Sparrow opened his eyes and realized Melonotha was carrying him toward the door. Behind him he heard the sound of fighting. Melonotha shoved him against the door and fished the access chip out of his pocket, slamming it into the slot by the door.

"Come on," yelled Melonotha. Sparrow looked back down the hallway. He could see that they weren't going to make it. Guards had joined the workers, and they were carrying guns. He looked around, saw the light juncture box, and lurched toward it. This was going to hurt.

Yanking his belt off, he ripped open the panel to the juncture box and shoved the metal belt buckle into the heat transfer juncture, then shoved the other end of the belt into the capacitor. Power arced through his body, and the lights flared from sapphire blue to blinding white. The Moliter all screamed and dropped to the ground, covering their eyes. Melonotha picked him up and hauled him through the door. Chafre and May sprinted after them.

Chafre slammed the door closed and, using an acquired shovel as a weapon, destroyed the door lock. In response, the automatic safety mechanism sealed the door.

"You crazy mother *fjandinn*," said Chafre. "Don't you know that skít can stop your heart?"

"You wanted me to leave you?" asked Sparrow.

"Shut up," said May.

"It was one swear," said Chafre, annoyed. "I'll put a credit in the jar."

"No," said May. "Shut up. I'm trying to hear this thing."

They all turned to look where May was pointing. The thing in question was about a meter tall, had four hands, and was red all over. He was wearing a pair of sandals, a loincloth, and a space helmet.

We are the Devil Ta.

Sparrow blinked at him. He was fairly certain that there was only one Devil here. He wasn't sure how that made a *we*, but he didn't have time to ponder the strangeness of a linguistic tic when there was so much else to react to. Up until now he'd hadn't heard anyone in his head besides Lina. She felt silvery and light. Ta felt sort of acidic and bright green. Which made no sense. He tried to respond to Ta the way he responded to Lina.

Sparrow.

Ta's attention immediately switched to Sparrow, and he grinned, a blinding white smile in his red face.

Well done. Your second mind learns quick.

Lina?

Too many guards. You go get help. This way. We take you to the surface.

Sparrow nodded. "Ta will take us to the surface."

"I almost heard that," said May. "Why can't I tune him in?" Her antennae waggled angrily.

"Use your second mind?" suggested Sparrow. Not that he had any idea what that meant. May gave him a To'Andan hand gesture that should have earned her at least two credits in the jar.

They followed Ta around a corner and found themselves in a wide corridor. Ta hopped up on a transport buggy and gestured for them to get in the rock hauler attached to the back. They did as he commanded and soon found themselves zooming upward along the steep arc toward the surface. When the gravity began to lessen, Sparrow punched in the hail code for the bracelet. The vast emptiness of space looming ahead of them indicated they were nearing the wide exit to the surface. Ta slowed the buggy and gestured for them to get down.

Sparrow lowered himself, trying not to feel the stabbing pain in his shoulder. The air here was even thinner than below, and he saw black spots at the edge of his vision as he moved.

The com bracelet flickered to life as the buggy began to move again. A small hologram hovered above the bracelet: the dark-skinned captain Sparrow had seen on To'Andan.

"I am Captain Carbanado. Identify yourself and give Ambassador Tum-Bel's location."

"My name is Sparrow Pandion."

"*Fjandinn,*" said Melonotha, recognizing Sparrow's name. Sparrow ignored him.

"I represent the Ránfuglar, and I was escorting the ambassador to her rendezvous with you when we were"—he glanced at Chafrc—"waylaid by the Moliter. She is being held prisoner within the asteroid. Can you home in on my signal?"

"Yes," said the captain. "What kind of threat are we going to find?"

"Several hundred armed guards, a few thousand civilian workers, and Count Talpidae. He's telepathic. Gifted. Whatever you people call it."

"Ah," said Carbanado.

"Do you have long guns?" demanded Chafre, leaning into the conversation.

"Not our business," muttered May.

"You said it yourself: *ástfanginn*," said Chafre. "Fire your long guns on the central node. It'll blow the port hub, and you can fly a small ship straight down to level five."

"Yes," said Sparrow. "Let's do that."

"We should warn the population," said Carbanado.

"He's torturing her, Captain. I no longer care about anyone on this damn rock. Pick us up at the surface in"—he checked in with Ta—"two minutes. If you want to give them that much warning, feel free."

Chapter 16:

THE AMBASSADOR HAS A DISCUSSION WITH THE COUNT

Lina became aware of a klaxon sounding. The room was filled with smoke. Her mouth was filled with blood where she'd bitten her tongue. She tried to remember the last thing she could remember besides pain. She had been with Sparrow and with the count. Mostly ignoring the count, but that had angered him and he'd adjusted the dial upward.

Men were rushing around. The count's daughter came into the room—she looked lost. She tried to attract her father's attention, but Talpidae shoved her against the wall, out of his way. He went to a monitor on the far wall and began to bark orders through the com system.

With his attention off her, Lina reached out again, this time to the girl. In response to Lina's prodding, she stumbled forward and began to undo the straps holding Lina to the Device.

Another alarm screeched, and in the distance she thought she heard weapons fire. Whatever had happened while she'd been absent had been bad for the Moliter. She supposed it was un-ambassadorial, but she felt happy about that.

The girl, whose name was Onyx, helped extract the needles and assisted her down from the machine.

Trying not to attract Talpidae's attention, Lina scanned the minds in the room and nearly laughed. The *Tempest* had blown out a central column, and then its small shuttle had flown inside. The explosion had locked down most of the asteroid as the inhabitants sought shelter behind emergency doors. Captain Carbana-do—who loomed like a dark fury in the mind of the guard she was scanning—Sparrow, and a landing party were making their way through the tunnels.

Unfortunately, Count Talpidae stood between her and rescue. Although the *Tempest* crew was trained and armed with a few technological innovations that no one outside of fleet headquarters was supposed to know about, Talpidae, with his massive cloud of power, was still managing to distract them and keep them lost in the warren of hallways.

That meant if she wanted to get off this damn rock, she was going to have to go through Talpidae. She reached out to the daughter's mind and pushed her slightly. Onyx took a step toward the machine. The count spun to look at her.

"Stupid child," he spat at his daughter. "Your mother was a useless whore to curse me with a daughter." He shoved a cloud of anger at her, and Onyx dropped to the floor, crying.

"That," said Lina, "is quite enough of that."

She could feel him pulling his thoughts away from the *Tempest* crew and Sparrow. She needed him to focus everything on her.

"Count Talpidae, I would like to inform you that I will be removing your daughter from your custody under interplanetary law regarding the mistreatment and psychic abuse of minors. Should you live through the next few minutes, I will also be placing you under arrest and you will be standing trial not only for your crimes against your daughter but also for the kidnapping and torture of an Alliance representative—to wit, me. We will also be lodging a formal complaint with your king and potentially levying sanctions against your people for the propagation of illegal mind devices."

Count Talpidae stared at her, his mouth hanging slightly open. Then he lashed out at her with a roaring fury and the full power of his mind.

The weight of it hit her like a hammer. She pushed back, holding up defenses already battered by his machine. Then she struck back at him sharply, stabbing into the place where he kept his fear.

He staggered back physically, clutching the console for support. She realized then that he'd never been on the receiving end. He was the essence of a bully. She made another strike, pressing her advantage. He summoned the cloud and hit at her. She felt a blood vessel in her nose pop but ignored the trickle of blood that ran down her face.

She rifled through his mind, looking for the things that would hurt. He could feel her doing it but didn't have the skills to stop her. He swatted at her again, hitting into her nervous system. She grabbed the machine to remain standing and crunched into his adrenal system, shooting adrenalin through his veins, and then pulled up a childhood memory of something called a Valga. Large teeth and six long, skinny legs hiding in the dark, waiting for small, warm prey, the Valga was the kind of thing designed for childhood nightmares. Talpidae screamed, pressing himself back against the wall.

Lina stepped forward and pushed hard on humiliation. Memories of pain tended to fade. They were never as effective as the real thing. But humiliation, that burned bright for an entire lifetime. She pulled up every memory she could find, from bed-wetting to insults in the king's court. She heaped them on his mind and manufactured one of her own—one of Onyx calling him weak.

"Never!" he screamed and launched himself off the wall, charging at her physically. He never reached her. Sparrow knocked him out of the air in a diving tackle. They rolled on the ground, coming to rest in front of Onyx.

The count focused on Sparrow, and Sparrow reeled away from him. Lina reached out, concentrating. She found feelings of defeat and failure and threw them at the count—drowning his mind in loss. The count sagged to the floor, his face going slack with horror. Sparrow managed to rise to his knees and punch the count once. Once was enough, and the count fell back, unconscious. Sparrow staggered to his feet and turned to look at Lina. He saw the expression on her face and turned back—but too late, as Onyx lifted the long, skull-piercing needle from the Device and drove it into her father's eye.

Chapter 17:

THE SPY ABOARD THE TEMPEST

He had been separated from Lina. Medics had swarmed him as soon as he was aboard the *Tempest*. He didn't understand why she wasn't beside him in the med-bay. What part about torture didn't they get?

He grunted as the doctor injected something into his shoulder. The pain immediately lessened and he was able to focus on the face of the woman leaning over him.

"Hi," she said. "I'm Dr. Katz. Do you have any medical conditions I should be aware of? Any religious prohibitions against receiving treatment? And how do you feel about experimental nanotechnology?"

"Yes, no, keep that skít away from me, and where the *fjandinn* is Lina?"

"I believe the captain was escorting her to the bridge," said Dr. Katz. "Not to worry. She's just fine. About your medical condition—"

"No," said Sparrow. He could feel Lina in his head. She was burning hot. "No, she's really not. Please send someone to bring her here."

"I'm sure if she needed medical attention she would say something. She doesn't like to be corralled into the med-bay right after a mission. It's better to let her sort things out and then check up on her. Don't worry about it. We have a system. Yes, I see from the scan that you have some interesting things going on with your back."

He tried to sit up and found that a force field was locking him in place.

"Now, hold still for a moment while we take this out."

There was a burning sensation as the metal pipe was extracted from his shoulder. He gasped, feeling the implants in his spine flare with pain, and yelled in agony.

"Hmm," said Dr. Katz. "Your pain levels just skyrocketed."

He had a few choice words to say on the topic, but he was concentrating on breathing.

"Let's just do a quick adjustment." Dr. Katz injected something else and the pain immediately lessened. He could hear her ordering additional scans, but at the moment all he could feel was Lina's fear of losing control.

"Hurry up, Doctor," he said.

"Somewhere to be?" she asked absentmindedly as she lowered something into his shoulder.

"Yes. I need to go get Lina."

She looked at him with amusement. "I really do assure you that she's quite safe."

"No. She needs to get someplace shielded, where thoughts can't get to her," he said.

"If there was a problem, she would let me know," said Dr. Katz soothingly. She began to apply other things to his shoulder, and little by little the shoulder went numb. "All right," she said, stepping back. The force field above him snapped off and he immediately sat up. His shirt had been cut off, and he saw the doctor blink at the scars on his back.

The med-bay doors slid open and a woman ran in. "You have to come!" she said, half-sobbing.

"Tola! What happened?"

"She wants Sparrow," gasped Tola, who he guessed was one of Lina's aides. "She pushed me."

"Pushed you?" The doctor stared at Tola in disbelief.

"In my head," sobbed Tola. "She made me come. She wants Sparrow."

"Don't say I told you so," said the doctor, looking at Sparrow.

"Show me," said Sparrow, dropping off the table. Tola nodded and ran from the room.

"Wait for me," called Dr. Katz.

Sparrow ignored her and ran after Tola. Katz caught up to him in the corridor and began to try to strap him into a sling as he ran. He pushed her off, but the lift was too confined for him to avoid her.

"She needs to get to her quarters," said Katz, strapping down the sling. "There's shielding there. Was it overuse? What happened down there? No one said she was injured!"

"There was a device," said Sparrow. "They took things out of her brain."

Katz looked horrified. "Do you know what things?"

"Chemicals. I don't know which ones. The count was a telepath. They were fighting."

"A duel? Like an actual duel? Holy Mother of Cordova. Uh . . . OK." Dr. Katz began to rummage in her medical case. "Tola! Hold this!" Tola obligingly held the case while the doctor began to slam things together. The door of the lift opened, and

Sparrow realized he no longer needed Tola. He walked down the hallway and finally found Lina in a crowded conference room. She was pale and had a white-knuckled grip on a chair back while Captain Carbanado argued with Captain Chafre. The count's daughter was cowering in a corner. The room was loud with voices, and he could only imagine what it sounded like in Lina's head.

"Enough!" he bellowed, and the room fell silent, staring at him in shock. "Captain, you need to decide these matters elsewhere."

"I think the ambassador—" The captain stopped when he looked at Lina. For the first time he seemed to take in her appearance. "Clear the room," he ordered. "Ms. Fina, escort our guests to their quarters. We'll decide where to take them later."

The first mate nodded and gestured firmly to Captain Chafre and his crew. They sullenly left the room with her. The other crewmen slowly filed out as well. Tola and the doctor arrived, panting slightly. The doctor immediately began to scan Lina, but Lina shied away from her hand.

Sparrow crossed the room and stood next to her. Gently he pried her hand off the back of the chair, and she transferred her grasp to his hand.

Room.

In her head there was a bed, and sleep.

"Yes," he agreed. "Tola, lead the way to the ambassador's room, please." He kept his eyes on Lina. She walked as though she was drunk—swaying slightly. The doctor continued to scan as they moved.

"OK, OK," muttered the doctor, rummaging again in her

case. As they reached the door, she shoved some vials into his injured hand. His good hand was still holding Lina's. "Make her take these. Lots of sleep."

The door closed behind them and Lina stumbled forward under her own power for the first time. Sparrow looked down at his hand. The doctor had given him three single-shot doses of something. He took out the first one and injected it into Lina's arm. She inhaled sharply but didn't move away. He injected the following two and looked around the room. It was a simple suite. Small living area, bedroom through the door to the left. Lina swayed and then turned and collapsed against him.

"It was so loud," she said into his chest. "I wanted to leave."

"But I need you to stay," he said, suddenly realizing what the stakes had been.

"Can we go to bed now?" she asked. "I'm really tired." That sounded like the understatement of the century.

"Yes. Only I have to get you out of your stupid wedding dress again."

She giggled and pushed away from him. He worked the buttons, not an entirely easy feat with one hand, and pushed the top off her shoulders and onto the floor. She leaned back into him and breathed out a sigh of satisfaction. Her next breaths were deep and sleepy.

"No," he said. "You can't sleep yet. I've only got one arm right now. I can't carry you."

"Right," Lina said, jerking upright. She stumbled into her room and flopped facedown onto the bed. He managed to roll her over and get her pants off. Both of them were covered in blood and asteroid dust. The sheets were going to be a wreck. He shrugged. Housekeeping problems were the very epitome of things he was not going to worry about right now. He stripped down and climbed into bed, and she immediately rolled over and wedged herself against his side. He wrapped his good arm around her and spared a thought of enjoyment at the luxury of a full-size bed as he drifted off to sleep.

PART IV:

Of Recovery, Family, & New Alliances

Then she laid her head on the bird's breast, but she was alarmed immediately, for it seemed as if something inside the bird went "thump, thump." It was the bird's heart; he was not really dead, only benumbed with the cold, and the warmth had restored him to life.

Hans Christian Andersen, Thumbelina

Chapter 18:

THE AMBASSADOR WAKES UP

Lina's head felt even worse than it had the morning after the diecohol. From the sitting room, she could see the ship lights indicating that it was day. She groaned and snuggled into Sparrow's side harder, hiding under the covers.

"Are you alive down there?" he asked when she didn't come back up.

No. Fairly certain I've been run over. I'm space debris.

"Sounds about right."

She pulled down the covers and tried to angle so she could see him clearly. Eventually she gave up and heaved herself on top of him so she could look down into his face. He'd obviously been to see the doctor. The bruises and cuts looked better. Not great, but better. He opened his eyes, and she smiled involuntarily.

"Do I pass inspection?"

Mine, yes. What did Katz say?

"I have no idea. She didn't have time to get around to a diagnosis before I had to go get you."

She felt bad about that. Or at least she would if she could remember much of it. The previous evening between the count and now was a bit of a blur. She tried to peer under the bandage on his arm.

But you feel OK?

She ran one hand down his side under the covers.

"Concerned for my health, or do you have plans for me?" he

asked, looking a little less sleepy.

Your health.

"Mm," he said, kissing her neck.

"I really was worrying about you," she protested, as his good hand slid downward along her back.

"But you could stop worrying and formulate plans if you wanted," he suggested, nibbling her ear.

"I suppose I could come up with something," she said with a giggle. He stopped abruptly and pushed her up a little, so he could see her face.

"Unless we shouldn't? What's good for recuperating tele-paths? Is sex permitted?"

"Yes, it's practically in the handbook."

"You have a handbook?"

"Guidelines and best practices. That kind of thing depletes the brain, and it's recommended that we do anything that pumps the brain up with positive chemicals like dopamine and sero-tonin."

"Well then, let me help you out with that," he said, kissing her again.

Such a gentleman.

An hour later they were lying on the floor, tangled in the sheets.

I don't understand how we have a full-size bed and still ended up on the floor.

Poor planning, he replied. "We started on an edge and rolled too much. We should have started in the middle."

Lina couldn't stop herself from chuckling. She stared at the ceiling and tried to assess her own brain. She really had thought she would feel worse. Admittedly, she felt rather bruised all over and seemed to be having trouble controlling her connection to Sparrow, but she didn't have the lingering depression and desire to curl up into a ball that she'd felt any other time she'd tiptoed up to the edge of her Gift. Instead she felt like a nap, a snack, and more sex. Not necessarily in that order.

Shower? she asked.

Room for two?

Lina considered that question. *Maybe?*

"Good enough," he said, standing up and helping her to her feet.

She was still drying her hair when the doorbell buzzed. In Sparrow's mind she could see it was the doctor.

Can you let her in? I'll be out in a minute.

She could hear the doctor and Sparrow chatting. Lina was going to have check with the doctor about his shoulder. She had no sooner thought the thought than she found herself drifting across the doctor's mind. Sparrow's shoulder was expected to make a full recovery; Dr. Katz was more worried about Lina. Lina grimaced at herself in the mirror and tried to pull her thoughts back before she was noticed. Popping into the heads of friends without permission was the height of rudeness.

She pulled on her robe and went out to talk to the doctor directly. Sparrow had disappeared into the bedroom.

Hi!

"Hi?" replied the doctor cautiously. "How are you feeling? I came to check on the pair of you."

"She brought clothes!" called Sparrow from the bedroom, and Lina smiled.

Surprisingly good. I feel like I should feel a lot worse. What did you give me last night?

The doctor hesitated, but answered. "The usual cocktail for overuse, plus a few other things I've been experimenting with."

Sparrow came out of the bedroom. He looked out of place in a set of ship's guest clothes.

Dr. Katz began to run scans on Lina, but she still looked awkward. Was she uncomfortable talking in front of Sparrow?

The doctor glanced up at Sparrow. "Sling! You can't keep it out of the sling for too long. It's too much stress on the joint." She pulled another apparatus from her bag and began to strap his arm down. She didn't seem uncomfortable doing that. Sparrow permitted the manhandling with a grimace. The scanner beeped and the doctor glanced over at it as she finished with Sparrow.

"Your levels are actually pretty good," said Dr. Katz, picking up the scanner and reviewing the results. "Particularly considering how bad you were last night. Did you do any of the recommended exercises?"

"Uh . . . We followed some homeopathic remedies."

"Really? Which ones? I should make a note."

Lina hadn't felt this embarrassed about sex since she'd walked in on her brother and his girlfriends. "Um," she said. Dr. Katz looked perplexed.

"She's trying to tell you we had sex," said Sparrow.

Sparrow!

"What? She's a doctor. Presumably she understands the mechanics of these things."

Well, I don't necessarily wish to discuss my mechanics with everyone.

"She's a doctor. Hardly everyone."

"Please stop," said Dr. Katz, holding up her hands. She looked faintly nauseated. "You're really freaking out my inner ear."

Lina was mystified. She looked at Sparrow to see if he understood any better than she did.

"She wants you to use your words, *sæta*," he said.

Haven't . . . "Haven't I been?"

"Sometimes," he said. In his head, she could see which particular times those had been. Lina blushed.

"My apologies, Dr. Katz," she said. "Apparently, while I feel passable, my control has definitely been affected."

"That's all right," said Dr. Katz, sticking her pinky in her ear and waggling it around. "To be expected, really. While I'm thinking of it: Mr. Pandion, you're going to calorie load for the next few days."

"What does that mean?" He was staring at the doctor in puzzlement.

"The treatment I'm using pulls a lot of its energy from your cells. Ordinarily I'd have you strapped into a drip feed down in the med-bay. But obviously, if you're insisting on . . . assisting in the ambassador's recovery, that won't work. It'll take longer this way, and you'll be needing additional food. Preferably high-calorie. High-sucrose is fine too, but try to get a lot of proteins."

Sparrow was about to reply when the com buzzed and Lina flipped open the channel from the desktop display.

"Good morning, Ambassador," said Captain Carbanado.

"Good morning," she said, conscientiously using her voice.

"I hope you're feeling better. We've been hailed by the Rán-fuglar." He looked past Lina to Sparrow. "Ránfuglarians?"

"Just Ránfuglar," said Sparrow. "It's already plural. The singular would be *Ránfugl.*"

"OK." The captain's face indicated that he was not planning on retaining that information. "Well, their ship is on approach. We should be within active com distance shortly. Did you want to come to the bridge for first contact?"

"Ah," said the doctor, shaking her head. "No. I would not recommend that. Strongly not recommend."

Strongly? You couldn't just stick with not recommend?

Dr. Katz shot her a dirty look.

"Unfortunately, I think Dr. Katz is probably right," said Lina out loud. "Do you feel comfortable handling it alone?"

"Yes, that shouldn't be a problem. But they've already inquired about Mr. Pandion. I expect they'll want to see him."

"Oh." she glanced up at Sparrow. "Of course they will."

"I'll come down," said Sparrow.

"On your own speed," said the captain, who signed off with a nod to Lina.

"I'll watch from here. Dr. Katz, was there more that you wanted?"

"Yes," said the doctor. "Don't think you're pawning me off with half a scan and threats of talking to me in my head."

"I'll be back up shortly." Sparrow dropped a kiss on her cheek and grabbed her com bracelet. He looked at her and she sent him instructions for how to call up directions to the bridge.

The doctor waited until the door closed.

"He seems . . ." She scratched her scalp. "Like none of my business," she said at last and picked up her scanner again. Lina waited while the doctor performed the scan. She could tell the silence wasn't going to last.

"You might as well just ask," said Lina. "Whatever it is, I can tell you're dying to."

The doctor applied the first of three injections and looked at her sidelong.

"There are some unique things going on with your brain chemistry. And I have to think that some of it is due to him. I don't suppose you'd let me run some active scans next time you and he . . ."

"No! Absolutely not!"

"Had to ask," said the doctor with a shrug, finishing the final injection.

"Go back to the med-bay or I'm not saying another word."

"It would be a boon to science."

"It would be an invasion of my privacy."

The doctor shrugged again, but her eyes twinkled. Lina shook her head. The com light flashed again, and she turned on the bridge feed as the doctor left.

She set the screen to split so she could watch her bridge and the one on the Ránfuglar ship at the same time. The woman on the screen was a vice admiral—assuming their ranking system was at all similar—and tall, with short red-blonde hair that reminded her of Sparrow. The more she stared at the woman, the stronger the resemblance grew. She cautiously extended her thoughts as the woman introduced herself as Vice Admiral Lilijasdottir.

Where is he?

Lina retreated hastily to her own head. The vice admiral was worried. Very worried. And the feeling of it clung to her.

The lift on the bridge of the *Tempest* opened, and Sparrow stepped out and went to stand next to Captain Carbanado. Even through the com connection, Lina could feel the vice admiral's wave of relief.

There was the usual patter of diplomacy. *Welcome. We'd be happy to escort you.* Platitudes and polite public words meant to go on record but kept to a minimum to avoid misinterpretation.

"We would also like to send a shuttle to retrieve our citizen," said the vice admiral, nodding at Sparrow. Lina cursed and was startled at the sound of her own voice in the quiet of her room. Of course they wanted him back. Why hadn't she seen that coming?

"Ah," said the captain, and Lina debated speaking directly to him. But her tiny venture into the vice admiral's mind had been overwhelming. Her friends and coworkers, people she knew better, would be even harder to block. She wasn't sure she could do more than exchange a few words over the coms safely. And using the coms could expose her and Sparrow to the vice admiral.

"Mr. Pandion is, of course, welcome to disembark at any time." The captain looked at Sparrow. "However, we had a recent incident involving the ambassador and a Moliter Device"—the captain practically spit out the word *device*—"and Mr. Pandion is proving to be of great assistance to our doctor in the ambassador's recovery. We would request that he stay. If possible." Apparently, the doctor had already sent word.

The vice admiral looked from the captain to Sparrow. The worry was back. "We hope that everyone is uninjured?"

"Everyone will recover," said Sparrow firmly, and Lina once again felt a wave of relief. She never should have tried to reach out. It was far too soon. "We just need more time."

"In that case, we are happy to do anything to assist in the ambassador's recovery. Mr. Pandion"—she said the word *mister* as if it were funny—"we will see you on Ránfuglar Prime."

The ships signed off and Lina pulled up an image of the vice admiral. She had to be Sparrow's sister. Lina was still looking at the image when Sparrow returned. She found herself promptly flinging herself at him in an embrace. He looked surprised, but happy to accept it.

"Sorry," she said, still hugging him. "I think this is from your sister."

"What?"

"The vice admiral is your sister, yes?" she asked without letting go.

"That was Finch, yes."

"She was really worried about you. Also, different last names?"

"She uses Mother's name. It's traditional."

"Tommy and I do too. Interesting."

"How worried was she? Is the hugging going to stop soon?"

"No, this is just me now. I like it."

Sparrow laughed and leaned back to look at her. "Well, if it comes down to it, so do I."

She looked up at him with his red-gold hair, blue-so-blue

eyes, and dimple next to his crooked smile, and felt her heart contract. She was so relieved that they hadn't been able to take him away yet. The weight of that thought settled in her mind, and she stepped back.

"We're in trouble, aren't we?" she asked.

His thoughts went about six different ways, one of which was that children might be nice. She didn't have time to pursue that one. Eventually they settled to a simple interrogative.

What?

"This was only supposed to last as long as the *Ember*."

"I know," he said. "But . . ." But he didn't want it to stop. She didn't even have to be Gifted to see that. "How long will you stay?" he asked.

Lina felt a prickle of tears behind her eyelids. "We usually stay to conclude negotiations and wait for an Alliance representative. There's some time. Six months, maybe."

He nodded and then smiled, and she could feel him making himself OK with that because he was used to not getting what he wanted. And that was more than a little bit crushing.

"Well," he said, "we'll just have to make the best of the time we have."

Chapter 19:

THE SPY RETURNS HOME

It was weird to see the flagship docked. It filled most of the port, dwarfing the smaller commercial vessels. He wondered if Finch was doing it on purpose to impress the Terrans. As he approached the gangway, the guard there maintained his position, eyeing Sparrow's Terran clothing with suspicion. Sparrow couldn't blame him.

The guard wordlessly pushed the ident-pad forward, and Sparrow dutifully placed his palm on it. The pad beeped and the guard read the name.

"Sir!" he said, snapping to attention.

"No salutes for me," said Sparrow.

"Sir!" The guard restrained himself from saluting just in time, and Sparrow chuckled as he went past. He expected to be challenged as he went through the ship, but apparently the guard had messaged ahead. As a result, he thought Finch would be prepared for him. Instead, he found Finch's quarters a disaster and Finch crawling on the floor in her underwear and a T-shirt.

He tiptoed into the room. "Lose something?" he asked, and watched Finch bang her head on the underside of the table.

"Son of a—Sparrow!" Finch crawled out from under the table, rubbing her head. "Not funny," she said as Sparrow laughed.

"Yes, it was," said Sparrow, and hugged his sister. Finch seemed startled and then hugged him back, tightly. "Not so hard!" yelped Sparrow. Finch stepped back automatically, her eyes wide. "Messed up my shoulder," said Sparrow, trying to rub the sting out.

"Sorry," said Finch, sounding genuinely apologetic. "Is it bad?"

"The Terran doctor thinks it'll be back to normal by the end of the week. So not that bad. Just try not to squish it, huh?"

"Will do," said Finch, relaxing. "What the hell happened out there?"

"What didn't happen out there?" responded Sparrow.

"We were worried when you didn't check in on time," said Finch, pulling on pants. Sparrow wondered which *we* his sister was referring to—the family or the fleet?

"There was a thing. We ran into some pirates. That's actually what I'm here about. Isn't your room usually cleaner than this?"

"I lost my damn pips," said Finch, looking around in frustration.

"What the hell are pips?"

"They're the things that go on the collar," said Finch, gesturing. "They tell everyone I'm important. I sent my uniform out to be cleaned for this afternoon's big to-do. I took the pips off, put them in their box, and now I can't find the damn things."

Sparrow laughed at her.

"It's all very well for you," complained Finch. "You don't ever have to go to any of these state things. And the arrival of the Terran ambassador is a big deal."

"I know it's a big deal! That's why I kidnapped her."

Finch stared at him. "Row, please tell me you didn't bring the Terran ambassador here with a gun to her head, metaphorical or otherwise."

"I'm kidding. Kidnapping implies that she wasn't jumping off a balcony when I found her. It was more a forceful extraction to avoid her having to marry the crown prince of To'Anda."

"I'd jump off a balcony too," said Finch. "When are you turning in your report?"

"I just landed!"

"You always delay. I might as well nag you now. What did you say about pirates?"

"Be'attle Corps. They're on the Terran ship."

"You want me to take custody and toss them in the brig?"

"No, I want you to give them a ship."

To her credit, Finch refused to bite on the bait. "Really? Any one of ours or just mine?"

Sparrow chuckled. "You're more fun when your head explodes and your eye twitches. I was actually thinking one of the confiscated ships we have in dry-dock. Nothing fancy. It's a three-man crew. Try to keep weapons to a minimum; we're only going to regret this later."

"We have a few that might work," said Finch, rubbing her hand over her head and making her short hair stand up. "Why are we outfitting pirates?"

"Because I wouldn't have made it off Count Talpidae's asteroid without them, and both the ambassador and I would be dead."

"You tangled with him?" asked Finch, her eyes wide again.

"Yes, but the good news is that no one will be tangling with him ever again." Finch's eyebrows went up. For once, he had managed to impress her. "Can you take care of the pirates? Also, we're going to need a nice dark room in a sanatorium for the count's daughter. Can you do that too?"

"Yes," said Finch with a resigned sigh, "as soon as I find my damn pips, I'll send some people over."

"Good," said Sparrow, reaching up to the top of the closet cabinet and pulling down the small black box that contained his sister's insignia.

"I hate you," said Finch, accepting the box as Sparrow chuckled. "Hey, what's the ambassador like?"

"You'll like her," said Sparrow. "She's funny. I'm going over to Mama's."

"Tan's going to want to see you."

"Yeah, but he's going to be watching your show with all the cabinet and everything. I thought I'd see him after."

"All right," said Finch, as Sparrow headed out the door. "You're going to need to come in tomorrow for a full debrief."

"Uh-huh," said Sparrow, leaving more quickly.

"And send in your damn report!"

His mother had moved to Widow's House after his father died, and Sparrow thought that all of his belongings were probably there. He hoped they were—he was going to have to find some clothes sooner or later.

He was about to knock on the door when it was opened by his mother's stiff-faced butler, Bernard. "Master Sparrow. So nice to see you." Bernard's head-to-toe inspection implied that Sparrow was looking far from nice. "Do come in."

Sparrow followed Bernard into the great room, where his

mother was sitting. She stood up and held out her arms. He hugged her tightly, lifting her off the ground, and she laughed at him. He suspected that Finch had called ahead because she avoided his injured shoulder.

"Oh my goodness, Sparrow," she said, stepping back to look at him. She reached up and touched his hair. "You need a haircut."

"Is it bad?" he asked, craning to look for a mirror. "I haven't exactly had access to a barber for about nine months."

"We'll get it sorted," she said.

"Can we get lunch sorted?" he asked. "I'm starving."

"It's barely after breakfast!"

"I've got a bum shoulder," he said. "The doctor said I'd be extra hungry until it healed."

He looked hopefully toward Bernard, who heaved a sigh and went toward the kitchen. The door opened and Tanager came in. Of the three of them, Tanager looked the most like their mother, with her auburn hair and hazel eyes.

"Tan!" He found himself surprisingly happy to see his irritating older brother.

"Row," said Tanager, smiling and stepping forward for his turn at a hug.

"I thought you'd be up at the palace watching Finch's thing," said Sparrow, noting that Finch had obviously called Tanager as well.

"I've got a few minutes. I wanted to hear what you've been up to. Obviously not a haircut."

"It's a little difficult to pop into a To'Andan barber," he said defensively and looked in the mirror again. Was it really that bad? Lina seemed fine with it. "I am going to need clothes, though. There's going to be parties and things, right? Do I have clothes?" He looked from Tanager to his mother.

"Yes, dear," said his mother, with a sigh. "They're in your room."

"I have a room? Didn't I stay with Finch last time?"

"Yes, dear," said his mother.

"Did you tell me I had a room?"

"Yes, dear."

"Never mind about that," said Tanager. "Tell me about the ambassador."

"You'll like her," said Sparrow. "She's smart."

"And whose side is she on?"

"The Terrans', of course. But she's definitely not on the Moliter side. She's talking about filing complaints and imposing sanctions." Bernard returned with a noodle dish and Sparrow seized it greedily. "Oh gods below, real food."

"Didn't they feed you on that Earth ship?" demanded his mother.

"Yes, and it was even pretty good for space food. But it's not"—he paused to inhale a mouthful of noodles—"actual food. Before that it was To'Andan Prime, and their food is horrible. I've literally been dreaming of that lasagna your cook makes with the little peppers."

"We'll have some for dinner," said his mother, looking amused.

"Can't," said Sparrow, swallowing. "Going back to the *Tempest* after Finch's thing."

"Why?" asked Tanager.

"We had a little run-in with Count Talpidae. The ambassador still isn't in tip-top shape. It'll be better if I'm there."

Tan went pale. "Is she all right? Are you all right?"

"Who's Count Talpidae?" asked his mother.

"The originator of the Moliter mind device," said Sparrow. "We're fine. Mostly. I should probably mention—" He tried to swallow. He hadn't expected to have to tell Tan this already. "She's telepathic."

"Oh," said Tanager. "Uh . . . that's not good." He could see panic setting in on Tanager's face.

"It's not like that," said Sparrow, annoyed.

"What's it like?" asked Mama.

"Think about standing in a room with about a hundred people yelling at you. And not about anything relevant. Just stuff. What they're going to eat tonight. What they think of your body, your clothes, your hair. The weather. What they feel. Just everything. And they won't shut up. Ever."

"Oh," said Mama. "That sounds horrible."

"Yes, that's what it's like for her if she can't shut people out. And after the incident with Talpidae, she's having trouble shutting the door. She needs more people who can shield around."

"So the shielding works?" asked Tan, looking encouraged. Sparrow nodded as he inhaled more noodles.

"She'll be better in a couple of days," Sparrow said, but then regretted it. He shouldn't have put a time limit on it. He might have been able to avoid suspicion longer.

Tan's coms beeped, and he glanced at it with a sigh. "I have to head back. You'll be around tomorrow, though, right?"

"Not going anywhere," said Sparrow.

"Good," said Tanager, hugging him again and then roughing up his hair. "Get a haircut," he said before leaving.

"You'll stay and watch the reception with me, though?" his mother asked Sparrow, turning on the display.

He nodded, still eating.

"You did warn her about the flying?"

"She knows we fly," said Sparrow, dropping into one of his mother's less delicate chairs.

"Yes, but did you warn her? I used to do these things with your father, and he always forgot. There's a difference between knowing we fly and having an entire flight wing descend on you. I still remember the poor Analysian ambassador throwing himself on the floor."

"She'll be all right," said Sparrow, grinning.

Minutes later the display showed Lina disembarking from the *Tempest*, accompanied by the captain and first mate in their dress uniforms. She had gone conservative with white clothing that displayed her dark hair and soft brown skin to an advantage.

"Oh," said his mother. "Sparrow! You said she was smart."

"She is. She's brilliant."

"Yes, dear, but smart is what you say about diplomats who actually got selected for their brains and talent."

He stared blankly at her.

"She's very pretty," she added by way of explanation.

"Oh," said Sparrow. "Then I probably shouldn't have told

Finch she was funny, either."

"No, dear. Here come the Flight."

A snap of wings was audible, even at a distance and through the display feed, as the fifty-some members of the Admiralty Guard descended on the flight deck in unison. The camera zoomed in, and for once Lina's diplomatic mask slipped. It was obvious that she was delighted. Sparrow suspected that this one moment would make his people love her. Now if only he could get his family to do the same.

Chapter 20:

THE AMBASSADOR DISCOVERS WHAT SHE'S IN FOR

At last they came to a blue lake, and by the side of it, shaded by trees of the deepest green, stood a palace of dazzling white marble, built in the olden times. Vines clustered round its lofty pillars, and at the top were many swallows' nests, and one of these was the home of the swallow who carried Thumbelina.

Hans Christian Andersen, Thumbelina

Lina flopped onto the couch and waited for Sparrow to come . . . She stopped herself before thinking the word *home*. The afternoon had been exhausting. Sparrow's sister, when the occasional thought had slipped past her defenses, had been hilarious and brightened the entire afternoon. But being that formal and in the presence of that many people thinking at her and about her had left her drained. She kicked off her shoes and pulled her feet up.

She hadn't realized she'd fallen asleep until she felt Sparrow come into the room. It was dark, and he was only a silhouette against the light from the bedroom as he bent over to brush her hair out of her face.

Hi.

She smiled sleepily up at him. It didn't matter that she couldn't see him. She knew where he was in her head.

"Hai," he said back. His intonation on the word sounded off—clearly it wasn't in common usage for the Ránfuglar. "Did you get something to eat?"

No. I think I fell asleep.

He picked up her arm and pushed buttons on her com bracelet. "You need some dinner, and I need second dinner."

"OK," she agreed, still not feeling quite awake. He was moving around the room—pouring himself a glass of water, taking off his boots. "Did you watch today? Finch and I did our best to be stately, but I rather think we may be the wrong people for the job."

He laughed. "No, you were both as stately as anything. Mama thought you were very pretty. She said I had to stop telling people you're smart or they'll think you're homely."

Lina snorted. "Did you have a nice visit with your mom?"

"Nice visit with everyone, actually. Hugs all around. Apparently, when you bring home a Terran ambassador everyone is pleased with you."

Lina chuckled. He came to sit on the couch, and Lina pulled her feet out of the way. He was silent for a moment and then cleared his throat. "We do need to talk about something, though."

Lina jolted awake. "You're breaking up with me?"

"No! Wait, what is breaking up?"

"When couples stop being couples!"

"Oh. That's what I thought. No, we're not doing that. We call that flying apart."

"I like that. Very descriptive. But then don't say *we need to talk.* Breaking up is the only thing that ever follows *we need to talk.*"

"No, it's not!"

"Well, nothing good ever comes after it!"

Mentally she could feel him conceding the point. "Sorry, let me rephrase. I need to tell you something because I think I forgot something important.

"OK?" She felt suspicious.

"Finch gave you packets of info on us and whatnot, yes?"

"Yes, but I haven't gone through any of it. Why?"

"Well, uh, I really should have mentioned it when you saw Finch, but by then I'd forgotten you didn't know. It's about my family and their jobs."

"It's fine. It's not embarrassing. My brother is a rear admiral. Mom was a fleet admiral. Admiralty happens to the best families."

He choked a little on the water he was drinking. "Yes, thanks. Actually, it's about my brother."

There was silence, and Lina reached out. He was feeling very awkward. Was Tanager the most embarrassing brother ever? What in the galaxy did he do for a living?

"Tan has the same job as my father. And my grandmother. And her mother."

She sat up and fumbled for the light by the couch. She had a bad feeling about where this was going.

"Tan's, um, well, Tan's the king."

She snapped on the light and turned to look at him.

"Oh my gods, you cut your hair."

"Yes, but don't you want to talk about—Do you hate it?"

"I can't deal with the other thing right now. Your hair!"

"Mama was insistent. I can grow it out again if you hate it."

"I don't know if I hate it. What will stick up at me in the mornings now?"

"Well," he said, and then didn't complete the sentence because she could see exactly what he was thinking. She leaned across the couch to run her fingers through his hair. He scooped his arm around her waist and pulled her onto his lap.

"You realize people are going to think I slept with you to get your planet into the Alliance?" she said, running her fingers through his hair.

"Or that I slept with you to get the Alliance here," he said. "Not very flattering either way."

"I don't hate it," she said, at last. "You really should have mentioned the king thing."

"I was working up to it, and then stuff got in the way."

He had stopped thinking about the conversation and was running his finger down the fastener on her top.

"Wait," she said.

He paused, lips inches from her breasts.

"That means you're a prince."

"Yes," he agreed, and continued on with what he'd been doing.

"That's going to take some getting used to," she said.

"You'll manage."

Chapter 21:

THE AMBASSADOR ATTENDS A PARTY

Lina smoothed her dress and took a deep breath. It was a party. Just a party. A boring diplomatic function. She'd been to dozens. But none of them had contained Sparrow's entire assembled family. Sparrow had assured her that they were not aware of the extent of his relationship with her, but she was still anxious to make a good impression. Eventually they would be bound to find out, and she wanted to garner as much favor as she could.

The doors swung open and she led the Alliance party into the ballroom. The ballroom was covered in glass through which the clouds of the planet could be seen, tinted orange and pink in the sunset. Half the base seemed to be in attendance. The dresses were ornate, and Lina felt a qualm about having selected a sleek one in a pale blush. Except that somewhere in the crowd was Sparrow, thinking she looked amazing.

The guests were assembled to face the door. Tanager was in front, flanked by Finch and the Head of the Congress. On Finch's side, a few people back in the arrangement, Lina finally spotted Sparrow standing next to a beautiful older woman she guessed was his mother. Lina offered her greetings, and the king responded. She suspected that had she not known Sparrow as well as she did, Tanager would have been hard to get a *reading* on. Although most of the Ránfuglar had the same easy unaffectedness to their surface thoughts as Sparrow did, digging deeper was difficult. She had assumed at first that they were blocking her, but three days in she was beginning to suspect they had some sort of natural defense. Which made her connection to Sparrow even more strange. Tonight Tanager seemed relaxed, and his confidence that the evening would go well put her at her ease.

Tanager escorted her to the dance floor to begin the festivities, and she felt Sparrow's jealousy like a sigh against her skin. She had reviewed the dance ahead of time. It was a basic waltz, and she had been relieved that it wasn't a complicated quadrille like the one she'd experienced on the Veraboran home world. That one had left her dizzy and relying on telepathy to get her through the next step. The formalities settled, she could feel the assembled guests relax.

Then Tanager escorted her over to Sparrow to formally introduce them. She could feel Tanager's amusement as they pretended to have their first meeting. Finch, however, seemed determined to torture her younger brother and promptly stepped forward and invited Lina to dance.

Lina accepted, and Sparrow stopped just short of snorting.

"Sparrow credits you for solving one of our linguistic mysteries," said Finch as she led Lina onto the floor.

Lina looked at her, questioning.

"Birds! Small feathered animals that fly. He says he and Tan and I are all named after birds and that in the old settlers' tongue *Ránfuglar* are also birds."

"I'm not entirely clear on *Ránfuglar*, but from his description, I believe it means birds of prey, possibly."

"But that's fascinating," said Finch. "Do you have pictures? Can we see our birds?" She said *birds* as though he were savoring the word.

Lina smiled. She liked Finch's enthusiasm. "Yes. We'll show you when you come aboard for a tour."

"Right! I'm looking forward to that. Your cooling systems look exciting."

Lina chuckled. "I'm glad you think so. I'm sure D'lan, our chief of engineering, will be happy to spend as much time on the cooling system as you could possibly want. Possibly more."

"But you'll be attending something exceedingly important elsewhere while he does?" asked Finch with a grin.

"I don't know what it will be, but it will be vital that I go handle it," agreed Lina.

"You know, I hadn't expected you to be quite so open with your tech," said Finch, giving her a spin.

Sparrow was liking her turn around the dance floor with Finch even less than he had liked the one with Tanager. "It's our policy to use share-tech as much as possible on these trips. For most of the systems you're interested in, we can provide specifications."

"Really? That's fantastic. Do you have a schematic on what you did to my brother?"

"What?" Lina's eyes flew to Finch's face, trying to *read* her.

"Do you know how long it's been since he walked into one of these parties willingly? Did you tie him down and show him pictures of dancing while feeding him opioids?"

Lina laughed. "Yes, that's exactly what we did. It's a sadistic form of brainwashing that forces someone to enjoy small talk, fancy clothes, and ridiculous canapés."

"That's not fair. For canapés, ours are entirely reasonable."

"You're the family flirt, aren't you?"

"Yes," she agreed. "Tan is the family brain. Row is the troublemaker, and I'm just incorrigible."

"How does Sparrow make trouble?" She was offended on Sparrow's behalf.

"You've met the man. When is he not in trouble?"

"That's a bit unfair," said Lina. "He's only been in all the same trouble as I've been."

"Then perhaps you're a troublemaker too," Finch suggested with a twinkle in her eye.

"I don't make trouble. In fact, I give people every opportunity to not cause problems."

"They just don't listen?" Finch was grinning.

"I believe you may be causing trouble right now," suggested Lina, putting on an air of offended dignity.

"Yes," she said. "I did mention incorrigible, didn't I?" Lina gave up and laughed. The dance ended, and Finch whirled her around with a flourish. "Come and meet Mama. She'll also want to know what you've done to Sparrow."

"I really haven't done anything," protested Lina. Nothing that needed to be made public, anyway.

You made him happy.

She tried not to trip as the thought popped out of Finch's head. Before she could address that in any way, she found herself being presented to Lilija Pandion. She was a tall woman with auburn hair and striking hazel eyes, and Lina felt that she was regarding Lina with pleased excitement.

Barely two sentences into the conversation, Finch wandered off, and Lina could sense Lilija's amusement at her middle child's lack of grace.

"I have been fascinated by your fashion choices," said Lilija, changing topics as Finch left. "The children do not seem to appreciate how difficult it is to dress for political events without an official uniform. I adored the dress you wore to your meeting with Tanager."

"Thank you," said Lina cautiously, checking Lilija's sincerity. The compliment seemed honest—a rarity at any diplomatic function. "There's been talk for years in the Ambassadorial Corps about putting together an official uniform, but there's been resistance because we don't want to be associated with the military."

"I can understand that. But it still must be a challenge, particularly when you must travel with a limited wardrobe. I said something about it, and they all just gave me that look."

"The one that says, *what alien speech are you babbling*?" asked Lina, thinking of her own brother.

"Yes," said Lilija with a smile. "That's the one. They don't appreciate the choices we have to make." She gestured to a waiter, and Lina accepted one of the offered cocktails. It looked elaborate and came decorated with a flower.

"It's beautiful," she said, smelling the drink. "It's wonderful to see so many organics."

"The flower is edible as well," said Lilija, sipping her own drink. Lina was about to follow suit when Sparrow snatched the drink out of her hand. She blinked up at him in surprise. His mind was only saying, *no, no, no.*

"No," he reiterated out loud.

"Sparrow!" gasped his mother.

He lifted a different drink from the waiter's tray and put it into her hand. "Yes," he said. "No diarvin."

"Ah," said Lina.

His mother looked horrified. "It's all right," said Lina, trying to smooth things over. "I can't have anything diarvin-based. It turns out I'm . . . uh . . . allergic. So unless you want to have me awkwardly passed out on the floor in twenty minutes, this is for the best."

"There was incident," said Sparrow.

"How frightening!" Lilija looked concerned.

"You're telling me," said Sparrow. "I thought I'd killed her."

"I was speaking to the ambassador," said his mother tartly. But she wrapped her arm around his in a small, affectionate gesture. "You should not have been so careless."

"I can't get any sympathy," said Sparrow, and Lina laughed. Affection for one another flowed around all of Sparrow's family. She liked how they all wanted to hug Sparrow. She frequently wanted to do the same, so at least they had that in common.

"And you'll get none! You could have warned us. We could have put a different drink on the menu. Should we be warning the other Alliance guests?"

"No. Pretty sure it's just me," said Lina ruefully. "Which is sad, because I actually quite liked the taste."

"Oh," Lilija said sympathetically, then looked past her. "Sparrow, what in the name of the seven stars is Finch doing?"

"Talking to that horrible woman you hate," said Sparrow.

"She is not horrible," said Lilija. "She's just wildly inappropriate for your sister to be seen with. Can you go do something about that?"

"For the record, this is why I hate these things," he said.

"You'll have to forgive my children," said Lilija. "Manners have never been their strongest quality."

"I like them," said Lina. Lilija looked at her sharply. "I have been informed that Tanager is smart, Finch is incorrigible, and Sparrow is a troublemaker, and those are three of my favorite types of people."

Lilija laughed. "Well, in that case, I'm sure you'll enjoy your stay here." She moved the conversation to less personal topics and swept her along to introduce her to a panoply of Ránfuglar political and social dignitaries. Lina was feeling in her element and felt in general that the party was a success. But she was mid-conversation with a rather pedantic engineer who was holding forth on wing shape—a topic that, while it was fascinating, he was managing to make boring—when she felt Sparrow panic.

The feeling lasted a split second, but it was a deep jolt of psychic dread. She pivoted toward the feeling, searching the crowd for him. She found him near the dance floor, talking to Dr. Katz and a round-faced man she didn't recognize. She sent out a feeler, a tiny question. He looked up and shook his head with an apologetic face. Whatever it was, he wasn't in any immediate danger. She took a deep breath to settle herself and turned back to her conversation only to find Lilija watching her with an expression akin to fear.

"Are you all right?" Lina blurted out, her hand reaching out impulsively.

"Just fine," said Lilija, stepping out of reach, her expression slipping back to polite kindness. "I was just thinking how nice it was to have Sparrow . . . back." Lina felt Lilija's meaning was deeper than being glad Sparrow had returned home, but when she reached out, she found that the older woman had slammed up all her defenses.

"Yes," Lina said, uncertain of how to respond. "But he doesn't have to leave again any time soon, does he?"

"Who can say?" said Lilija. "I didn't know he was leaving the first time, or I would have hugged him more."

Lina glanced at Sparrow, still in the crowd but coming their direction. "Always time for hugs now," she offered.

"Yes," said Lilija, still eyeing Lina with a wariness that Lina couldn't account for.

The rest of the party passed without incident, and when the end of the evening arrived Lina retreated to the *Tempest* with relief. Sparrow arrived a few minutes after she did, stepping through her cabin door already stripping off his jacket.

"Get me out of this thing," he said, tugging at the buttons on his shirt. "I feel like such an idiot."

"But you look so handsome," she said, complying and running her fingers down the shirt seal. The shirt opened—the buttons were just for show—and she slid her hands inside to run along his skin.

"Then it was worth wearing," he said, leaning down to kiss her. "By the way, bets are being placed. They're offering even money on you and Finch."

"What?" Lina stared at him in disbelief.

"You laughed at her jokes."

"She's funny! I also laughed at that poor man with the truly bizarre hair."

"Donald. Don't bring up the hair. There's a pool running on how long he'll keep it that way. You could affect the odds."

"But—" said Lina, and he kissed her. "No, seriously." She broke away. She could feel him laughing at her. "Oh, and I thought this evening went so well," she said, distressed. "Between this and that weird moment with your mother, now I'm worried."

"Yes, Mama caught us," he said, looking unconcerned.

"What? Sparrow! How?"

"Something about the way we looked at each other. I don't know. She asked. I said yes. I'm not going to lie about it."

"Mm," said Lina.

"You're worrying," He kissed her again. "Stop worrying."

"I am worrying," she said, even as her body leaned into his. "I want your family to like me."

"They do like you," he said, unsealing her dress and kissing along her exposed bits.

"And what about earlier—you were worried at the party. Why were you worried?"

The kissing ceased, which wasn't what she had been trying for. "Your doctor wants to speak to my doctor."

"About what?" she asked, tightening her arms around his neck, holding him to her.

"What else? My back injury. Katz just said she wanted to make sure nothing she'd done had interfered with my implants. I told her it was fine, but then she went and found my doctor, so now it's a thing. He's coming by in the morning."

Lina felt a tight knot of worry in her stomach, and she couldn't tell whether it was her worry or his. She knew she should be focusing on the upcoming negotiations—the Alliance needed a win; this was important—but all she could think about was Sparrow. And he was all she thought about for the next several hours.

Chapter 23:

THE SPY IS SURPRISED BY HIS FAMILY

The next morning, he left Lina preparing for her negotiations with Tan. There had been a good-faith exchange of informational packets. The two civilizations knew so little about each other that they couldn't even negotiate for terms without finding out what there was to negotiate for. Lina's team was poring over the documents and studiously ignoring Sparrow, although he rather thought they were biting their tongues. He could tell it went against the grain not to pump him for information.

He went down to the med-bay and found the doctors already waiting for him. He was stripped of his shirt, and the medical techniques used to heal his shoulder were gone over. He felt, as usual when on a doctor's table, like a slab of meat married to an interesting problem. Muscle matrix, skin enhancements, nanites, digital frame—the terminology washed over him, and he reminded himself to breathe, to not clench his fists. This was the easy part. The hard part would be when it came to his spine.

"Well, that is all fascinating!" exclaimed Erlandson. "I can see why you wanted to consult with me. Once you discovered the cybernetics and the bionic implants, you must have been concerned about any nanotechnology you were considering."

"Yes! You see the problem. The idea of introducing anything mechanical into his system . . . it could have been disastrous! But his reaction to the biological growth matrix is, I think you have to admit, encouraging."

Katz pulled up the 3-D model of Sparrow's spine, and both doctors turned away from him to inspect it. Sparrow knew very well what it looked like. His spine was a jigsaw puzzle of crushed vertebrae and repurposed bionic implants, controlled by the cybernetics in his skull. After the accident, no one was sure how the cybernetics had reconstructed the bionic implants to carry the workload of his spine. Erlandson believed that Sparrow had done it himself, willing the implants to change. The engineers the family had consulted all said the same thing: don't touch it. They feared that any adjustment might undo what had been done. So Sparrow had endured the hypersensitivity that came with the slow physical adjustment of metal within his body and along his spinal column. For two years everything that touched him had been a fire on his skin. Even after the nerves had calmed down, he would still experience occasional jolts of pain from an unexpected touch. He'd endured it because walking was worth it. The fact that he couldn't fly again was a torture, but at some point, he had to simply be grateful that he could go to the bathroom without help. The fact that he was no longer able to touch people regularly was simply the cost of the cure. The metal pieces coiled in and around his spine made living possible, but not always fulfilling. Until he'd met Lina, he'd assumed that it never again would be.

"It was well received, but I'm not sure how far you can push the technology. What point are you trying to think of repairing? The spurs here along C6?"

"No, the whole thing," said Katz. "This technology can rebuild bone. We could replace the missing vertebrae. My question is, how will the cybernetics react? Could they simply be replaced or re-tasked back to their original purpose?

Sparrow felt the world swim in front of his eyes. He couldn't hear Erlandson's reply because he was too busy trying to breathe. He could feel Lina before she arrived. She was hurrying.

"What are you doing?" she demanded, stepping through the med-bay doors practically before they opened. "Stop it, right now!"

Erlandson and Katz both turned to her in surprise and Sparrow got off the table, already realizing the problem.

"I'm fine," he said as she flung herself at him.

"You're not fine," she said, her voice muffled from the way she was pressing her face into his chest. "What are they doing?"

"They are discussing my spinal problems," he said. She turned her head but refused to let go of him, so he pivoted so she could see the model of his spine.

"Holy space sprites! Is that your spine?"

"What's left of it, yes," said Sparrow. She blinked at the model and then back at him, then worked her fingers along his spine. He heard Erlandson inhale in fright, but Sparrow didn't feel any of the previous nerve pain. He never did with her.

"Huh," she said. "You have a metal octopus for a spine. Exciting."

"I don't know *octopus*," Sparrow said.

"It's an eight-legged sea creature of extraterrestrial origination, with no skeletal structure, that can fold itself into practically any shape."

"Surprisingly apt," said Erlandson, still staring at the way Lina's hands were resting on Sparrow's spine.

"I would like it to be less apt," said Katz. "I think we can regrow some of the vertebrae, but I'm unclear how that would affect the cybernetics or the bionics. It's a delicate balancing act in there. Obviously, we don't want to detrimentally effect anything, but I think we do have a chance of making improvements."

"And I think I would like to see proof of concept before you even think about touching him," said Lina, sharply.

"Well, yes," said Erlandson, clearing his throat. "We would have to run extensive tests and modeling. We'll need an engineering team. And I rather think the king would have my head if we were to go about this without a certain level of certainty. But at minimum the idea is exciting."

"Exciting," said Sparrow. "Sure. That's one word for it." He glanced at the clock on the med-bay wall, now adjusted to local time. "*Sæta*, we both have to go get ready."

She looked around at the clock, frowning. "We're coming back to this," she said, looking from Katz to him.

"I suspect we'll be coming back to this a lot," said Sparrow, tiredly. He wasn't sure he was prepared to dive back into the miasma of doctor's appointments and surgeries.

"The answer can always be *no*," she said, looking up at him. "It's your back."

He shook his head with a smile and kissed her. "Go get ready. Tan's expecting us."

"Don't think you can use some sort of intergalactic alliance on which the fates of potentially millions of people depend just to avoid talking about your health."

"Wouldn't dream of it," he said with a grin.

"Mm," she said, but her eyes twinkled. She kissed him again and left.

"Doctor Erlandson," said Sparrow, pulling on his shirt, "if you would be so kind as to not mention anything you just saw until after the negotiations are complete, I would appreciate it."

"I'm not sure," said Erlandson, clearing his throat. "Your brother—"

"Will be a lot less annoyed if it comes from me."

Erlandson nodded his fervent agreement.

Sparrow let himself into his mother's house by the back way, hoping to avoid notice. Not that anything was ever totally unobserved at Widow's House, but at least he could avoid her butler's judgmental gaze. He bounded up the stairs, feeling his spine flex in response to each movement. He wasn't sure what to think about Erlandson and Katz's plan for his body, but the idea of flying again . . .

He opened the door and was halfway through when he realized his entire family was assembled and glaring at him.

"At least now I know why you've been avoiding writing your report this time," said Finch.

"Mama! Seriously? You had to tell everyone?"

"Yes! It's a matter of national security!"

Sparrow rolled his eyes and then realized that wasn't helping his cause any. "Yes," he said, shutting the door and trying to remember that he wasn't seventeen. "Of course it is. But I find it rather insulting that you don't think I'm aware of national security interests. And I have been working on the report," he said to Finch.

"In your spare time," remarked Finch.

"What little there is of it, yes. It's just that the report is a bit long."

"Your last report was two paragraphs and full of drang *skit*," said Tanager, drily.

Sparrow was startled. He wasn't aware that Tanager read his reports. He assumed Finch did, which was why he occasionally included bits that would make his sister laugh. Individual reports from operatives rarely made their way to the king's desk.

"Well, this one is up to four pages. You can pull it up if you really want to read it. It's not done, though, which is why I haven't submitted it."

Finch grabbed her tablet and began to tap.

"You're really checking?"

"Yes," said Finch. Sparrow restrained himself from rolling his eyes again and went into the kitchen to build himself a sandwich. He winced as he pulled open the bread drawer.

"You said you were seeing the doctor this morning. You said you were all right!" His mother's voice was sharp with worry.

"I am fine," Sparrow snapped, then took a deep breath. "I actually just forgot I was injured. Erlandson and Katz both gave me the green light. I should be back to normal, or whatever they're calling it, in a day or two.

"You let Erlandson look it over?" Tanager asked, looking relieved. Sparrow wasn't sure what to make of Tanager's mood. He would have expected more yelling.

"Yes," said Sparrow, and this time he couldn't keep the annoyance out of his voice. "Do you want to check on that too? I left him on the *Tempest* trying to decide how to test—" He looked up from his sandwich ingredients. They were staring at him. "Never mind. I'd rather talk about Lina."

"I think I'd rather talk about your doctor," said Tanager. "What did they want to test?"

Sparrow sighed. They were going to find out anyway. Tanager would just call Erlandson into his office and that would be the end of it. "The Terran doctor can apparently regrow bone and some tissues. They thought they might be able to replace some of my missing vertebrae." They stared at him. "They want to run some tests to see if it's feasible and how the implants would react."

His mother sat down abruptly as if her knees had given out. "I can't do this," she said. "I can't. You've been gone so long and I can't, Row. I just can't."

"Can't what, Mama?" he demanded impatiently. "You don't have to do anything. It's my spine."

"I'm not talking about your spine! It's been ten years and you've barely touched any of us, and now you're home and you smile and you hug me and I can't go back to the other way. I'm not going through that again!"

Sparrow stared at his sandwich components. That was the real reason she was worried about Lina. It had nothing to do with national security and everything to do with him.

"What do you think?" asked Tanager. It was probably the first time he'd ever asked Sparrow that question. "Is that really something they can do?"

"I think it's really . . ." He hesitated.

"*Ógnvekjandi,*" muttered Finch, without looking up from Sparrow's report.

Sparrow didn't want to admit that *frightening* was probably accurate, so he ignored the comment. "If it's possible, it's exciting. But I'm waiting until they actually have something to look at before thinking about it too much."

Tanager nodded.

"She's going to go away," said his mother.

"What?" Her sudden change of topic threw Sparrow off balance.

"She'll go away, and then you'll be . . ." His mother waved in a hand gesture that expressed nothing but her distress.

"She's right, Row," said Finch. "There will be the negotiations, and then they'll probably send a permanent representative. Assuming things go well. But that's six, seven months, tops."

"Yes," said Sparrow, putting his sandwich together. "That's about the number we came up with."

"Yes, but—" Finch looked around the room or support. "I mean, that will be . . . hard."

"Yes," agreed his mother. "You have to stop this. Before you get hurt."

Sparrow slammed the jar of peppers on the counter. "Some things are hard. Some things hurt, they always hurt, they don't get better. When are you going to get that through your heads?"

His mother inhaled sharply but didn't answer back. Finch and Tanager exchanged looks. Sparrow took a deep breath and looked back at his sandwich.

"What were you thinking?" asked Tanager again. "Were you

planning on taking the relationship public?"

"I was planning on waiting until after the negotiations and asking you what would be best for you."

"Public would seem better," said Tanager, and their mother made a shocked noise of protest. "The press always sniff these things out."

"That's what I thought," said Sparrow. "But I didn't know what you would think."

"You missed a section," said Finch, still reading Sparrow's report. "You went straight from the asteroid blowing off a chunk of the exterior paneling to *repairs were completed.* How'd you manage that?"

"Dura-Shield putty and the shirts off our backs," said Sparrow. "The To'Andan material mixed with nebula gas will harden under cold heat. In case you're interested or ever have to repair a spaceship with only six sheets of Dura-Shield."

"You both could have died!" exclaimed his mother.

"Finch! I have told you not to read those to Mama," said Tanager.

"Are they all like that?" Their mother looked wide-eyed.

"No, this one is a little more exciting than usual," said Finch soothingly. "What'd you do about gas and radiation exposure? I packed that ship myself." Another thing Sparrow hadn't realized. "There wasn't enough for two detox baths."

"We shared," said Sparrow. There was silence in the room, and he saw their faces as he picked up the sandwich. "Oh, what? You already know we're sleeping together. Shared detox bath is what shocks you?"

"I just hadn't realized that she was quite so . . . adventurous," said his mother.

"You thought being kidnapped and tortured by a Moliter mind device wasn't adventurous?" asked Sparrow around a mouthful of sandwich.

"Spoilers!" exclaimed Finch. "I haven't gotten to that part yet!"

"What do you mean, *spoilers*? You were there at the end. I told you."

"Well, yes, and I appreciate knowing that you live, but I like to find out how you got there on my own."

Sparrow continued chewing and ignored Finch. "Tan, you should ask Lina and Dr. Katz about the mind machine. They may have some treatment ideas. And alternatively, they may have some ideas about how to stop the machines."

Tanager sort of nodded, appearing to still be thinking. "If she leaves, will you go with her?" he asked. Sparrow scratched his ear and tried to finish chewing. Tanager's mood was starting to worry him. There really should have been yelling by this point. Dad would have been purple in the face and out of breath.

"No," he said. "I wouldn't have a job on her ship. I think that would about kill whatever we've got."

"Would she stay?"

"She's not opposed to it, but she'd probably have to quit her job," he said. "I don't think she's the stay-around-the-house type either."

Tanager nodded.

"Tanager!" snapped his mother. "Why are you even considering this? Tell him to fly apart from her!"

"No," said Tanager. The family attention now switched to him. "He wouldn't do it, for one. And for another, while yes, this complicates matters, it certainly predisposes her to look more kindly on us."

"That won't mean she'll be any kinder in negotiations," said Sparrow.

"There are negotiations and then there are . . . extras," said Tanager. "Negotiations are the letter of the law. Extras are things like access to her doctor."

"No," said Sparrow, feeling as if Tanager had opened a chasm under his feet. "Do not . . . This isn't about me."

"You're right, it's not. We have several operatives who've been destroyed by the Moliter mind machine. And as you just pointed out, the Terrans might be able to help. If they are so inclined. And there are other, similar intangibles."

Tanager wasn't helping. He was looking at too many of the angles. Lina wasn't an angle. "I'm not sleeping with her to help you!"

"I didn't say you were," said Tanager calmly. "I'm saying this is the situation I've been presented. There are pros and cons. And I have to determine what's worth getting upset about and what's not. At the moment, what's worth getting upset about is the fact that we are thirty minutes away from a negotiation that could change the course of our people's lives and you have tomato blobbed down your shirt and haven't showered.

Sparrow looked down at the mess on his shirt.

"So if you are coming with us, and I had hoped you were,

then I really wish you would do something besides shovel food into your face."

Sparrow thought about arguing with Tan, because that felt like what was expected. But Tanager had just rather explicitly agreed to not put up a fuss about Lina. Maybe he should take his win and shut his mouth. Sparrow grabbed the sandwich plate. "On it," he said, heading for his room.

Fifteen minutes later he was dressed and looking more or less presentable as they walked to the Blue Room. Tanager was looking regal. Finch was looking noble. Sparrow suspected that his appearance was letting the family down.

"Tan," he said, craning to look in a mirror. "Have I got this right? I haven't worn this damn suit in forever."

"You've never worn this suit," said Tanager, straightening the collar. "Mama had it made when I told her you were coming home."

"Oh," said Sparrow, looking down at the suit. "No wonder it didn't look familiar."

Tan continued to straighten. "I'm not Dad, you know."

"I have thought that on more than one occasion," said Sparrow.

"For one thing, I actually will punch you," said Tanager, and Sparrow grinned. "I'm just saying"—he managed to get the collar where he wanted and stepped back to inspect it—"I wish you would stop leaving."

"Stop sending me places," said Sparrow.

"You would have left anyway," said Tanager. "At least when I send you places, I know you have to come back. You know, if you don't get yourself killed first."

Sparrow found that he had no response for his older brother. It was a little like pushing on a door and expecting it to stay closed but then falling flat on his face when it opened. He didn't know how to react to this Tanager. Apparently, being king had changed Tan more than Sparrow would have thought possible. Tanager patted Sparrow's collar. "All right, when we go in there, please remember that there will be reporters. Try not to do anything embarrassing."

"And now I'm back to thinking you're Dad," said Sparrow.

Tanager grinned. "We all remember the drang pupae incident—that's all I'm saying."

"You put me up to it," said Sparrow, still outraged twenty years later.

"Yes," admitted Tanager for the first time, "I did. Although I blame Finch."

"I'm not involved in this," said Finch, coming over to check her uniform in the mirror.

"You're the one who procured the pupae!" It was Tanager's turn to look outraged.

"I don't know what you're talking about. I have no memory of that. I think you're both delusional."

"I'll punch you too," said Tanager. "And I'll get away with it because I'm king and you two suck."

"No, you won't," said Finch calmly, turning back to the mirror. "Because Mama would yell at you. And also because that would embarrass us in front of Row's new girlfriend."

"She'd probably laugh," said Sparrow. "She has a brother too."

"Just the one?" asked Finch. "Lucky woman."

Chapter 24:

THE AMBASSADOR NEGOTIATES

Lina watched as the array of Pandion siblings walked into the room. They were well worth looking at, and as a set they were quite dazzling. Next to her, Tola, her diplomatic aide, let out an audible sigh, and Lina clamped her teeth together around a giggle. She was Earth's representative at the moment, and laughing was not the way to go down in history. Lina had to admit that she rather thought she had picked the best one.

The introductions were made, the portraits created, the greetings extended. Tanager, unlike some of the other colonial representatives she'd worked with, had the ease of a polished statesman. He knew exactly how to sound and look engaging and approachable yet still better than the next person in line. He was confident; she didn't even need to *read* him to know that. These negotiations were important to him, but he wasn't nervous about them—he wasn't expecting to be surprised.

Lina stepped forward and gave her usual speech. She'd changed it up a little, given her more personal experiences in the nebula. Disconcertingly, she could see the number of viewers tuning in at any given time in a ticker above the camera. It was holding steady at nearly the entire population. Then Sparrow helped her down from the podium and escorted her to the negotiation table. She repressed the urge to kiss him publicly. Cameras always brought out her rebellious side. She could feel, even without a formal *reading*, that he was also repressing a fit of laughter, and she avoided eye contact. He seated her at her place and then went to his side of the table to sit with his siblings. The reporters filed out, and the room relaxed.

"That seemed to go well," said Tanager, flipping open a tablet.

"Yes," Lina agreed. And decided now was the time to upend his confidence. "Before we begin—and I'm rather sorry about this, because the agenda was so tidy—but I would like to bring some new information to the table. Do you mind if we discuss it now? Or should I lodge a formal request?"

Tanager hesitated, and specifically didn't look at Sparrow. "We can discuss it now."

"As you know, my team and I have been preparing for this meeting. There has been some discussion with your people and much of it has centered around the planet. You project that it won't be habitable for another five hundred years, is that correct?"

"That is the current estimate," said Tanager.

"I spent this morning hogging a dreadful amount of time on the communications satellite to speak with the head of terraforming in our Department of the Interior. I think I may have just spent our entire communications budget for the month." Lina shook her head in dismay at the terrible number of credits she'd blown through for a real-time conversation. "But after showing him some of the information you released to us, he was of the tentative opinion that with our assistance the timeline could be significantly sped up."

"How significantly?" asked Tanager.

"Obviously, terraforming is not my area of expertise, and you will need to have your experts speak to him, but he seemed to think that with the progress you've already made it could be habitable within seventy-five to a hundred years."

There was an audible gasp around the room.

"I understand that part of the reason the Ránfuglar are interested in joining the Interplanetary Alliance is the military pressures and threats surrounding the planet. But at this point, I would like to point out that terraforming services can be purchased independently of joining the Alliance."

"But they could be provided as a benefit to joining the Alliance, along with military support?" asked Tanager.

"Yes, that could certainly be part of the joining agreement," said Lina.

"And what would that cost us?" asked Tanager.

"The standard joining agreement that would we sent would still be in place," said Lina. "We would expect some additional considerations."

She eyed the siblings. Finch was looking distinctly uncomfortable. Tanager had his eyes narrowed as if running a large number of internal calculations. Sparrow's mind had moved into action mode.

"No," said Sparrow. "I read that agreement. The tax rate? Too high. We would expect that waived outright for three hundred years and then have an escalating rate for the next hundred after that."

"Two generations? No tax for two generations? No planet in the Alliance is getting that!"

"No other planet in the Alliance is brand new," countered

Sparrow. "The transition to planet living is going to be difficult and expensive. We're not going to pay that rate."

Lina restrained a grin. He was ridiculously sexy when telling her no. She was going to have to find other things for him to negotiate.

"Sparrow is correct," said Tanager. "We're not going to pay that rate. I also read over the briefing. The Alliance has many bases. It needs planets. But more to the point, it needs planets that produce resources. If the Alliance taxes us right away, it'll be a dead end for both of us. We're bringing new technologies, new crops, and a new planet to the table. I think there's room to negotiate."

Lina smiled and flipped open her tablet. "There is always room to negotiate," she said. "Shall we begin?"

The clock had struck midnight by the time the negotiations finally wound down. She had to admit that the Pandion siblings made for a formidable opponent. They each spoke to certain topics of expertise, and Tanager melded it all into an overarching and amazingly educated viewpoint that allowed him to make decisions almost at once. Where other leaders would have had to ask experts or refer back to others, Tanager compressed the decision-making down to himself and shortened what could have taken weeks to mere hours. It was a marathon of negotiating, and Lina was tired by the time they all stood around the table, checking over their lists and reconfirming what they had decided.

"I think that's it," said Lina, looking over Tola's notes.

"No, it's not," said Tanager, looking from Sparrow to Lina. Everyone had their defenses well up, and she could only sense that he was trying to tell her something. She looked at Sparrow for assistance. He looked equally blank.

"As discussed on the subsection about territorial oversight, the Alliance will be posting a permanent ambassador to this region."

"Yes," said Lina.

Tanager looked at both of them again and then, in what was possibly the most brotherly expression she had seen him make to date, sighed in exasperation. "The Ránfuglar request approval and rejection rights to this posting. And furthermore, we would like to formally nominate you for the position."

"Oh," said Lina.

"Yes," said Sparrow, as if his brother's words were a revelation. "Yes, we definitely want that."

"*Hálfviti*," Finch murmured, glancing at her brother.

Lina was the one who felt like an idiot. She hadn't even considered that angle. She tried to assess what that would do to her career. It was a jump forward in title but a jump back in prestige. Unless she could get the nebula trade going again. Current estimates, assuming that she could wrangle agreements with all parties, had the nebula pipeline producing within the next ten to fifteen years. She could probably beat that. Particularly with Sparrow's help.

"Yes," she said. This was going to be so much fun. "Yes, we accept that."

Tanager grinned and held out his hand to Lina. "We're in agreement then?"

"Yes," she said. She shook his hand, but she couldn't stop looking at Sparrow.

Chapter 25:

THE AMBASSADOR AND THE SPY TAKE FLIGHT

When he saw Thumbelina, he was delighted, and thought her
the prettiest little maiden he had ever seen. He took the gold crown
from his head, and placed it on hers, and asked her name, and if she
would be his wife, and queen over all the flowers. This certainly was a
very different sort of husband to the son of a toad, or the mole, with
his black velvet and fur; so she said, "Yes," to the handsome prince.
Then all the flowers opened, and out of each came a little lady or a
tiny lord, all so pretty it was quite a pleasure to look at them. Each
of them brought Thumbelina a present; but the best gift was a pair of
beautiful wings, . . . and they fastened them to Thumbelina's shoulders,
so that she might fly . . .

Hans Christian Andersen, Thumbelina

Lina tiptoed to the edge of the platform and looked out and down. Below her the pink clouds of the planet puffed by, unconcerned with her nerves.

"I can't believe you talked me into this," she said, reaching out to hold Sparrow's hand.

"I talked you into nothing," said Sparrow. "I said it was possible and you jumped up and down and yelled *yay*."

"If I crash and die that is not at all how I'll be telling it," she said, looking up at him. The sunrise gilded his hair to bright gold and his new wings to rosy silver.

Two years as the Alliance ambassador to Nebula Six and she felt the same about Sparrow as the day she'd taken Tanager's hand in agreement. Every morning arrived with a sense of glee that she was waking up next to him. And a year ago, when he said that he'd convinced Tan to allow her to have the bionic implants that would permit flight, she had been ecstatic. There may have indeed been some jumping and yelling.

Behind her, the wings Sparrow had commissioned for her fluffed nervously. They were replicas of her tattoos, and she loved them. But staring over the edge of a platform into nothing but thin air, she found her confidence diminishing.

"Did you pick the highest platform to start from?" she asked, looking over again. The test flights had all gone well. Why was she so nervous? Maybe Sparrow was nervous?

She checked her feelings. Sparrow was nervous! Why was he nervous?

The doctors still hadn't made any headway on why she and Sparrow had maintained their psychic link so strongly even after her recovery from the Moliter Device. There were some theories about the diarvin extract, but privately Lina suspected that it was either because Sparrow had a low level of telepathy or, more likely, simply because neither of them wanted to stop.

"Well, yes, actually, it is the highest flight platform," he said. "I figured if I scared you half to death, you wouldn't be thinking clearly when I asked you to marry me, and then you might say yes."

She stared at him in disbelief. He grinned impudently and stepped off the platform. His wings snapped open, catching the wind, and he spiraled upward.

"Sparrow!" she yelled in fury and launched herself after him.

Her wings caught the wind and she inhaled the scent of the air produced by the planet below. It smelled of salt and a little of the ocean. Somewhere below the clouds a beach was forming. A beach that perhaps her—their—children would walk on.

"Sparrow!" she said, breathlessly, arriving at his level.

"Will you?" he asked, flying closer, a tricky maneuver that she was not yet skilled enough to emulate. "Marry me?"

"Yes," she said, and he kissed her, their wings brushing together for a moment in the light of the morning sun.

The End

WANT MORE FROM THE GALACTIC DREAMS UNIVERSE?

WHY NOT TRY...

by

J.M. PHILLIPPE

PART I:

The eleventh one had just pronounced her blessing when the thirteenth one suddenly walked in. She wanted to avenge herself for not having been invited, and without greeting anyone or even looking at them she cried out with a loud voice, "In the princess's fifteenth year she shall prick herself with a spindle and fall over dead." And without saying another word she turned around and left the hall. Everyone was horrified, and the twelfth wise woman, who had not yet offered her wish, stepped forward. Because she was unable to undo the wicked wish, but only to soften it, she said, "It shall not be her death. The princess will only fall into a hundred-year deep sleep."

Jacob And Wilhelm Grimm, Little Briar Rose

Chapter 1

Moargan Royal Guard Riska Dvorak felt a drop of sweat run down his spine to the small of his back and resisted the urge to wipe off his forehead. He knew his pale skin was likely flushed red, the freckles on his face popping out more in contrast. There were too many people in the audience chamber, and the atmosphere regulator wasn't doing enough to compensate for the excess body heat. Still he did his best to not fidget while doing his regular visual sweep of the room. His twin sister, Royal Guard Eva Dvorak-Camacho, wasn't having as much luck standing still, and was shifting her weight from foot to foot as though it hurt to stand, her long red braid swinging softly with her movement.

I knew it was too soon for her to come back, he thought. He had pushed back on her request, but she went over his head to Queen Sulina, who had graciously granted her favorite attendant her request. Eva had been very smug about it too. Riska knew Eva had just done it so that she could see all the festivities taking place on the naming day of the royal princess. Her own daughter, Stacia, had her naming day just two weeks before, an intimate celebration of close friends and family. If Riska had his way, that's the kind of affair he would have planned for the princess as well security at an event like this had been a logistical nightmare. The flower displays and hanging ribbons all seemed designed to create blind spots in his visual field, even if they were pretty. Still, they weren't half as bad as the giant hats and overflowing skirts that many of the guests had chosen to wear. The room was dotted with the colors of all twelve provinces, although the green, blue, and black of Moarga were the most prominent color combo.

Riska told himself that he had taken every precaution that could be taken, despite protestations from the Queen, but he was still nervous he missed something. Being assigned to the princess was a promotion, one he still wasn't quite sure he earned. Still, guarding an infant couldn't be that hard, once the celebrations were over at least.

Riska let his gaze float back over the crowd. He was standing at the edge of a dais centered at one end of the audience chamber. The walls curved out away from the dais, and the floor slanted slightly up the further from the dais it went, all to allow the maximum number of people to view Princess Chavri in her bassinet next to the Queen's chair. It was quite a view, as the princess had taken after her mother with tawny skin and a mass of dark brown hair she had been born with. Her dress in the royal colors of blue, green, and black plaid brought out the green in her hazel eyes. She was a remarkably pretty baby with dark lashes and full pink lips, and her even temper had already won over the crowd. The bassinet had been slightly tilted up, and the sides were lower than usual to also allow maximum view and easy access on the times that the Queen needed to pick her up to present her to some lord. She was sleeping now, despite the sounds and sights all around her, and adorable with her hands fisted up by her face.

The King stood on the Queen's other side and did his best to give a heartfelt speech of thanks for every gift presented to his daughter. A tall man with skin lightly tanned by the sun and thick chestnut hair he kept shorn short, the King made an imposing presence on the dais, the famous Aisling blue eyes sparkling every time he looked at his daughter. The Queen's pride was quieter, revealed in a small smile that never seemed to leave her face. Her beauty had become Chavri's beauty, with the same tawny skin and dark hair and lashes. The Queen's eyes were dark brown though, so dark they almost seemed black, and were all the more striking for it.

Eva was on the King's side of the dais in a position mirroring Riska's and completely in view of the crowd of courtesans filling the room. Eva had asked for that spot specifically, in order to see as many of the gifts as possible. The Queen granted that request as well, liking the symmetry of her two red-headed attendants framing the dais in their matching uniforms of blue and green jackets over black trousers and boots.

Riska bet Eva was regretting her request now though. They were in the third hour of gift presentations, and even his feet were starting to hurt, and he hadn't given birth just over three months ago. Thankfully the delegation from Durrant, the last of the eleven other provinces, was presenting their gifts to the princess, which improbably included a small boat carried in on the shoulders of six of their citizens. What they thought a three-month old was going to do with a boat was beyond Riska, and he looked over and caught his sister's eye to see if she was as amused by this as he was. She was shifting her feet again.

"You're fidgeting, Eva," he said into the microphone in the headpiece hanging off his right ear.

"I'm fine," she said back, and he could see in his peripheral that she was now still.

"It's almost over," he said. "You've handled it like a champ."

"I am a professional," she chided. "Don't think that motherhood has changed that. And I can still kick your arse. Probably."

Riska chuckled, and heard matching chuckling from various others stationed around the room. It was an open line, but the group was used to the Dvorak twins chatting along it.

"I'd bet on her," Mel said, managing to hide the fact he was speaking by putting a hand in front of his mouth. As the King's dedicated guard, he was standing on the dais, slightly behind and to the right of King Ardan.

"I'll take that wager," Nora chimed in from her position behind Queen Sulina's chair. "If anything, motherhood will give Eva an edge." She was speaking from personal experience, having birthed a child two years ago who had been the darling of the royal guards until Eva's little Stacia came along to bask in the shared attention.

"What do you say, Eva, when should this go down? After dessert?" Riska glanced sideways at his sister and tried to keep himself from smiling. Guards weren't supposed to show any emotion.

But Eva's attention was caught on something else, something that Riska couldn't see. Riska tried to follow where her eyes were looking, but the damn boat was blocking him.

"Eva?" he asked.

"A movement. Something." Her voice was tense.

Riska turned his attention to the crowd's feet on the other side of the boat, looking for any change in their general movement or other sign that something was amiss. There: a set of shoes darker and heavier than the others around them. Riska moved his gaze back to his side of the room and found at least three other pairs of shoes as dark and heavy as the first. They were just shoes, part of his brain told him, but his hand moved to the plasma gun at his side, and his instinct knew that something was definitely wrong.

"Look for dark boots," he said, keeping his tone low so that only other guards could hear him. "Thick heeled. Outside wear. Black or brown."

He was riding a fine line between acting appropriately and overacting, and the last thing he wanted was to create panic in the room and cause some sort of stampede.

"I've got eyes on two sets," he heard Eva say through his ear piece.

"Three up by the Mehmtok contingent," Nora said.

"Two more near the folks from Durrant," Mel added.

The sweat that had been pooling at the base of Riska's spine seemed to turn to ice. He pulled his gun and instinctively jumped up on the dais, moving swiftly toward the princess.

"Alpha response!" he shouted, every instinct in him telling him to get to the princess as soon as possible. The guards positioned throughout the chamber immediately jumped into action, pulling guns and looking for trouble. The mysterious boot-wearing folks threw off cloaks and revealed weapons underneath, and people throughout the chamber screamed and tried to head for the double doors in the back.

Just then, a hand-sized cylinder came soaring out of the crowd, arching down toward Chavri's bassinet. Riska realized with horror that it would land before he could get to it, and he pushed his legs to move faster. He saw Mel drag the King from his chair and away from the bassinet, while Nora had a harder time pulling the Queen away due to her awkward position in the chair between the King's and the bassinet.

The canister bounced off the edge of the bassinet, landing somewhere inside and expelling green gas. Riska took in a deep breath and held it as he lunged forward. The canister was lying next to Chavri's feet, the number thirteen engraved on the metal, and he reached in and grabbed it. His hand instantly felt like it was on fire, but still he kept his grip, pulling the canister out of the bassinet and flinging it to the other side of the dais where the least number of people seemed to be. In the next moment, he swept the princess up in his arms, noting that Nora finally had the Queen pulled away, and that Eva was waving people back from the canister, which was still smoldering and expelling gas.

Riska held Chavri tight to his chest and ran toward the back of the dais, protecting her with his body. Her screams were muffled against his shirt, but he took comfort that at least she was still breathing. He didn't stop until he had her safely ensconced in the reinforced throne room, a force field barrier and a line of guards between the royal family and anyone that would attempt to attack them. Riska looked down at the princess. She was still crying, which was a good sign, but her color was too pale, and there was a tinge of green around her mouth and nose.

Her doctor snatched her from his hands, and Riska finally let go of his breath, taking in deep gulps of air after his run. He saw then that the Queen had collapsed on a small couch and was coughing and choking, her own mouth slightly green, a doctor running a scanning instrument over her. Only the King seemed untouched by the gas, but his guard Mel was on the floor, vomiting violently. Riska looked down at his burned hand, and saw that the flesh looked sick, like it was necrotic. The number thirteen was burned into his flesh.

Eva! The last time he had seen her she was waving people away from the canister, the same one that burned him, the same one that he threw—toward her side of the dais. He pushed past the nurse who was trying to scan his hand and shouldered a few other guards away until he got to the force field.

Nora, the queen's bodyguard, stood between him and the controls.

"You can't," she said. "We have to keep the seal."

"Eva's out there," he said. "I need to get to her. I left her out there. I left…"

"You saved the princess. You did your job. And Eva did hers."

He tried to push past her again, but Nora stood firm.

"I have to get to her," he said again. "I have to…"

But there was something about the way Nora was standing, the sadness in her eyes.

Nora put her hands on Riska's shoulders then, forcing him to look her in the eye.

"She did her job. She saved the royal family. She saved a lot of people. I need to you to hear me. I need you to understand. She did her job."

Riska blinked at Nora several times, cradling his burned hand to his chest.

"She did her job," he repeated, still not fully understanding what Nora was saying.

"She did her job," Nora said back, softly. Then Riska finally understood. He collapsed hard on his knees so suddenly that Nora had no chance to hold him up, and fell to her knees with him.

"No," he said, shaking his head. "No, she…no. She has a baby. Little Stacia. No."

Nora nodded, keeping her hands steady on Riska's shoulders.

"She did her job," she said again. "I saw her do it. She just threw herself down on the canister, covering it with her body. She didn't hesitate. She didn't falter. She did her job."

For a second hope bloomed in Riska's chest.

"Then she might be, she might…"

Nora shook her head, her eyes directing Riska to the proof in the room: Mel, who was still vomiting, the Queen, who was being rushed away on a stretcher, and even Riska's own burned and dead-feeling hand. If Eva had thrown herself on the canister, she wasn't going to survive the experience.

"I'm so sorry," Nora said.

Riska felt it then—the burns, the fear, the adrenaline, and the grief, all at once. His shoulders shook and his head fell forward, heavy tears streaming down his face as he wailed.

AND COMING IN 2019

by

Bethany Maines

PART 1:

The Swans & the Queen

The children, seeing that someone was approaching from afar, thought that their dear father was coming to them. Full of joy, they ran to meet him. Then the Queen threw one of the shirts over each of them, and when the shirts touched their bodies they were transformed into swans, and they flew away over the woods.

The queen went home very pleased, believing that she had gotten rid of the children. However, the girl had not run out with her brothers, and the Queen knew nothing about her.

Jacob and Wilhelm Grimm, The Six Swans

Chapter 1:

KEELIA BLACK AND THE END OF THE BLACK LIGHT

Keelia Black of the Swan Clan watched through the domed glass of the hanger deck as her ship, the Black Light, exploded in a fiery blossom, beautiful and silent against the inky blackness of space. In front of her, Easton, her second oldest brother, dropped to his knees and began the Prayers for the Damned.

"You have just violated intergalactic law," said Niall, the eldest, his voice hoarse with rage.

Fang Nazari laughed. It wasn't a mad laugh. Or even particularly evil. Fang was delighted. As if Niall had promised her double desserts after dinner. "I know!" She drew a deep breath as if inhaling the smell of victory. "And wasn't it fun!"

Keelia turned and examined their captor more closely. Fang was nearly eight feet tall—either space-born or modified and she didn't walk so much as glide. Or perhaps it was her dress that moved? The fabric, if it could be called that, moved around Fang as if made of millions of tiny green iridescent insects. Occasionally bits of her dress broke away from the mass and crawled up into her turquoise hair and sometimes into her mouth where she ate them with an audible crunch.

Keelia and her six brothers, Niall, the twins Easton and Graves, Jedidiah, Anwell, and Mataxlen had arrived in the quadrant earlier in the week. Alliance surveys had indicated that it was uninhabited, but likely to hold profitable asteroids. The Black children had harvested two ice rocks and were looking for dwarf star alloy when their scans had picked up an asteroid the size of a small moon with multiple alloy pings. They had landed, prepared to do a survey, and a little exploratory digging with their father's newest invention—a sonic drill.

What they had found was a moon base, a mad woman, an army of robots and what appeared to be a seven foot man-alligator. Fang Nazari, as she had introduced herself had wasted no time in launching one of her robots, armed with a detonator and a cubic meter of the highly explosive dwarf star alloy at their ship.

And now their ship, and their way home, was dust and debris.

The circular hanger was a donut shape. At the center was a shaft dug into the side of the asteroid—meant for venting engine exhaust into space. A force field kept the atmosphere in the hanger deck and out of the shaft, allowing them all to breathe. Deep below them, Keelia could see that the turbines and grav-shields were inert. Meaning the shaft wasn't in use at the moment. She couldn't imagine what kind of engine would require a vent shaft that big. Above them, inside the shaft, exposed to space, a complex arrangement of scaffolding, handles and cables proliferated allowing only glimpses of the dark expanse of space beyond.

Around them stood an army of robots, led by the commands and tail flicks of the alligator looking creature that was almost as tall as Fang. He snarled at every move the Blacks made, but once their mistress had called a halt, neither he or the robots had moved.

Behind Fang stood three humans, none of whom had taken

part in the fighting. The first was a man with dark fringed eyes, thick beard, and long black hair, tied up in a knot on his head. He held his hands in front of him as if they were in chains, although no cuffs were in evidence. The second was a woman with broad shoulders and green hair. The third, an older man had white shot hair, red-rimmed eyes, and gnarled hands. All three of them were filthy with dark dust and watched the Black children with flat, impassive expressions, as if they had seen this show before.

"Your actions indicate that you would like war with the Alliance," said Niall. It was a stall. Everyone knew that this far out the law of the Alliance wasn't worth the data stream it was imprinted on. It was really just to give Easton time to make contact. Every morning the telepaths on each ship of the Swan Clan received an image of who the Swan Emergency Beacon would be that day. Today it had been their mother. Her hair, red like Keelia's own, vibrant in the rendering. Easton was attempting to calm his mind and send a distress call. They all knew what the odds were. Their mother was a very long way away and no one could possibly reach them for months. But at the very least the Swan Clan would descend in fiery retribution for their deaths.

"The Alliance doesn't exist here," snapped Fang. "There is only me or space. So now you have a choice. If you'll notice, there are escape pods around the room."

"Mat," said Niall, pointing at their youngest brother. Mataxlen jogged to the nearest pod, jostling past the cylindrical robots who creaked in protest.

"The pods are standard issue: enough fuel for a short directional thruster burst, twenty-four hours of air, and only short range communications," said Fang pleasantly. "Or so I'm told."

"Air and fuel tanks look full," said Mat running back. "She's not lying. Also, Dura-flex coating and a docking arm." There was an exchange of looks. Dura-flex coating was resilient, flexible and could withstand the outer corona of a sun, such as the one located a short distance from their position. A docking arm meant that the pods could be linked. Their possibilities for escape had just expanded.

Easton chanted softly, leaning against his twin's leg for stability.

"You got here in a very lovely, very large ship with a lot of air and fuel. I'm sure you know exactly how far those pods will take you," said Fang, smiling gleefully, unaware of the subtle shift of mood in the Black's. "I'm sure you will acknowledge that the pods are simply a prolonged method of suicide. But I do have another option for you."

"What's that?" asked Niall.

"Work for me," said Fang, crunching a piece of her dress between her teeth. "I'm in need of experienced diggers."

"Pods," said Niall, without hesitation.

Fang looked mildly surprised. "Interesting choice. You did hear me state twenty-four hours of air, right?"

"Pods," said Niall again.

"Before you commit I feel I should point out a few little… problems with the pods."

"Such as?" Niall's face had hardened into angular planes, his jaw clenched so hard that Keelia was worried for his teeth. Of all of them, he looked like a true Swan—thick white-blonde hair, light brown skin, aquiline nose and a square jaw. Her brothers were all variations on the theme—some more brunette than others, but all with the same blue eyes. She was the one who stood out with her mother's fiery red hair and her father's green eyes.

"Well, for instance, there is no internal release. In order to eject, someone has to manually release each escape pod. And of course, there is the fact that the release buttons are all inside the exhaust shaft." She pointed upwards.

"You mean, someone has to stay behind," said Niall.

"Is that what it means?" asked Fang with a wicked grin. "I should also point out that whoever stays behind would have to use this air canister and it only has three minutes of air." She patted a breather mask and canister next to her.

"Our suit tanks all had more air," said Niall pointing to the collection of canisters that had been ripped from their suits along with their helmets when they had surrendered.

"What tanks?" asked Fang, and the droids promptly began to crush the tanks in pinching claws, the tubes popping and leaking the air out in angry gusts.

"Right," said Niall."

"The other problem," continued Fang, "Is that the computer estimates that it would take someone five minutes," she traced an arc from right to left in the air, "to make it around the entire circle. "Five minute trip. Three minutes of air. You might want to factor that in to your decision making."

Keelia looked up at the path that Fang had traced. It made sense that the computer would estimate that route—it was the safest. But safest also meant slowest. She could do it faster. But how much faster? Within three minutes?

Niall turned his back to Fang and surveyed his siblings. Keelia did the same. They were all fighters. Even Jed, who was their medic, was a better fighter than she was. They all had more skills in piloting, flying and ship maintenance than she did. She did have one thing that they didn't. A childish talent based on stubbornness.

"Easton?" Niall asked.

Easton abruptly stopped chanting and stood up. "Mother says: *Quicquid capit.*"

They all nodded—they knew the family motto.

"Who stays?" asked Niall.

"That's me," said Keelia.

"Can't be you," said Anwell. "Everyone knows Dad wants to leave you the business." It was a family joke. Everyone knew Dad didn't have a business. He had a lab, mad dreams and crazy inventions that Mom turned into a business. Langston Black invented things. Rayna Black kept them all flying. Keelia had been the first in the family to go to an official school. She was only working with her brothers until the Engineering Guild reviewed her test scores and approved her license.

"I'll be faster," said Anwell. "I'll do it."

Keelia shook her head. "Yes, you and Niall are faster than me in low grav, but I can hold my breath the longest," said Keelia.

"The best shot for everyone is if I do it."

They all looked to Niall. She didn't have to add that she would be counting on them to come back for her. That was a given. Niall reluctantly nodded once and then all nodded together and began to move, running for their pods.

Niall hugged her tightly, for only a second.

"You stay alive," he whispered in her ear. "Whatever it takes."

Quicquid capit.

Then he was gone.

Keelia turned back to Fang who was watching open mouthed as the brothers dispersed. Behind her she heard the sound of running feet and the first pod slam shut.

"You must be just the biggest wet blanket at crew parties," said Fang, staring down at Keelia as if she were a new and disgusting form of mold.

Keelia steadied herself, trying not to feel the loss of her wall of brothers as she stared up at the pale face of Fang Nazari with her red slash of a mouth, and dark black eyes. Keelia didn't answer Fang. Her voice would probably shake anyway and she didn't want to embarrass the family. Fang would never know that she was scared, that her mouth was dry and her palms were wet inside her space suit. She marched past the towering woman and picked up the breather apparatus, weighing it in her hands.

Fang slid around in front of her, watching her with eager eyes. As if genuinely interested to see what Keelia would do next.

"Three minutes of air?" Keelia asked, looking up at the levers and buttons.

"Three minutes," said Fang reassuringly. Behind her, the man with the long black hair, shook his head in a small negative gesture and held up two fingers.

"Good to know," said Keelia, and strapped on the face mask.

Niall was stepping into his pod. Keelia tightened down the straps on the mask, started her watch and hit the oxygen apparatus to start the flow. Then she sprinted across the access ramp to the exhaust shaft and launched herself upward into space.

2019

ABOUT THE AUTHOR

Bethany Maines, a native of Tacoma WA, is the author of action adventure and fantasy tales that focus on women who know when to apply lipstick and when to apply a foot to someone's hind end. When she's not traveling to exotic lands, or kicking some serious butt with her black belt in karate, she can be found chasing after her daughter, or glued to the computer working on her next novel.

FIND OUT MORE AT:

BethanyMaines.com

OTHER WORKS BY BETHANY MAINES

www.ingramcontent.com/pod-product-compliance
Lightning Source LLC
Chambersburg PA
CBHW072105170626
46813CB00004B/1464